BOOT SCOOTIN' BOOGEYMAN

A HANNAH HICKOK WITCHY MYSTERY BOOK THREE

LILY HARPER HART

HARPERHART PUBLICATIONS

ONE

"Can you see me better now?"

Hannah Hickok looked up from the clothing items she was perusing and fixed her grandmother Abigail Jenkins, who just happened to be a ghost, with a pleasant — if distracted — smile. Her mind was elsewhere, but it wasn't every day that you got to hang out with a grandparent who had passed over so she wanted to be as accommodating as possible.

"I think you look the same," Hannah offered, her smile rueful. "Sorry."

"Darn it!" Abigail viciously swore under her breath, perhaps trying to keep the words that one wouldn't normally say in front of a grandchild under wraps. Hannah had excellent hearing, though, and she wasn't the type to be offended by a little cursing. Still, it seemed to be important to Abigail that she pretend she hadn't heard, so that's what she did.

"Have you considered that you're tired?" Hannah offered, holding up a blue shirt and shifting her eyes to the mirror. She'd been told the top was flattering at one time and she was trying to ascertain if it was appropriate for a date ...

because she actually had a date. She couldn't remember when she'd last had a proper date — it could've been never, since she never really dated her boyfriend in college, who became her fiancé (and then relentlessly cheated on her before the relationship ended with a screaming bang) — but she had one now.

"I'm a ghost," Abigail reminded her reasonably. "I don't think ghosts get tired."

"I don't think that's true." Hannah swayed back and forth in the mirror with the shirt held out in front of her. "I think it's like anything else. You have to practice, but you're still getting used to the fact that you're a ghost. Since it's a relatively new thing, you have to beef up your stamina."

"Or I could just do it well from the start," Abigail groused. She was focused on herself rather than Hannah so she didn't notice the critical eye her granddaughter was giving herself in the mirror. "I've always been good at things. This should be no different."

"I think you're being too hard on yourself." Hannah grabbed a pretty black dress from the stack of clothes she was considering and held it up. "Just out of curiosity, do you know where people in this area go on dates?"

Slowly, Abigail tracked her eyes to Hannah, as if noticing for the first time that the feisty blonde was focused on something else. "What do you mean?"

Hannah did her best to appear nonchalant. "You know ... dates. If a man asks out a woman, for dinner let's say, and they head somewhere else that's not a cosplay western town located on top of a mountain, where would they go?" Hannah shifted a pair of nervous eyes to the ghost. "And what would one wear to that establishment?"

Abigail took a moment to study the items in Hannah's hands and then burst out laughing. It wasn't the reaction Hannah was expecting.

"Are you and Cooper finally going on a date?" she asked when she'd recovered.

"Maybe." Hannah's turn was swift as she went back to looking in the mirror. "I don't know that I would use that word. I mean ... it feels dated. Ha, ha," she laughed hollowly. "The word 'date' sounds dated. That's weird, huh?"

"I don't think the word is dated," Abigail countered, moving closer to Hannah so she could meet her granddaughter's gaze in the mirror's reflection. Hannah had grown up separate from Abigail and they hadn't been blessed with a relationship of any sort when Hannah was young. They were still feeling their way around each other now, but their relationship was becoming more and more comfortable each passing day. Abigail considered it a blessing that she was getting to know her granddaughter at all and kicked herself for not realizing that Hannah had other things beside ghostly shenanigans on her mind today. It was obvious, now that she gave her a hard look, that Hannah couldn't have cared less about her ghostly staying power.

"You don't?" Hannah's mouth twisted into a grimace. "I don't know what to wear." She threw the dress and shirt on the bed and flopped down next to them, her eyes trained on the spinning ceiling fan above. "I think ... I think this might've been a mistake."

Abigail thought otherwise, but she decided to play the rational sounding board rather than the fervent cheerleader. "And why do you think that?"

"Because we work together." Hannah propped herself on her elbows. "What happens if we go out on a date and realize we hate each other? What if he chews his food too loudly or talks with his mouth full? What if he thinks I'm an idiot or I step into some unflattering light? That's going to make working together difficult."

"Sure. Sure." Abigail made a popping sound with her

ethereal lips. "What if it's the best thing that ever happened to you, though? What if he's charming — and, trust me, he is — and he makes your heart flutter in a way you never thought possible? I'm pretty sure he already does that last one, though."

"Yeah. That's the problem." Hannah grabbed one of the pillows and placed it over her face so she wouldn't be tempted to make eye contact with her grandmother. "I think I'm afraid."

"I think you are, too." Abigail's tone was soothing as she hovered closer to the bed. "You don't have to be afraid, Hannah. Cooper is a perfect gentleman. He's also strong, a good listener, and seems to be smitten with you."

Ugh. That wasn't what Hannah wanted to hear. She wanted someone to reinforce her fear and tell her it was okay to chicken out of the date. Apparently Abigail hadn't gotten the memo. "Smitten?"

"It's a word," Abigail countered. "It also perfectly describes what I see when you two are together. I don't see what you're getting so worked up about. You guys have spent an inordinate amount of time together since you arrived and it's clear you like one another. Besides, you've eaten a good thirty meals together and you would already know if he talks with food in his mouth."

That was a fact. In truth, Hannah felt comfortable around Cooper Wyatt, the head of security at Casper Creek, the Kentucky Western town that Abigail had left her when she died. When she was with Michael Dawson, the cheating fiancé from hell, she'd never felt comfortable in her own skin. She was convinced that was how he liked things. If he kept her guessing, she wouldn't be able to focus on everything that was wrong with the relationship because she was so desperate to make everything right.

Cooper, however, was the exact opposite. He liked

Hannah for who she was, warts and all. He didn't care that she'd only recently discovered she was a witch, complete with magical powers, and he found it cute when she stuck her foot in her mouth ... which was quite often. He was patient, explained things to her when they needed explaining, and was eager to spend time with her. He didn't make her beg for a few precious moments here and there. He happily volunteered hours upon hours.

"I think I really like him," Hannah muttered. The statement was more for herself than Abigail but there was no way the ghost didn't hear.

"I think you really like him, too," Abigail agreed, her grin mischievous when Hannah finally removed the pillow and met her steady gaze. "It's okay to be excited about a man. That doesn't mean you're not a strong female. It simply means you're more than one thing."

"I guess." Hannah forced herself to a sitting position and grabbed the shirt and dress. "Which one?"

"The dress," Abigail answered without hesitation. "It's not too fancy, but it will show off your shoulders and legs."

"Is that a good thing?" Hannah asked dryly. "I mean ... aren't you supposed to be steering me toward a non-sexual relationship? Er, well, at least until marriage."

"That takes the fun out of things, doesn't it?" Abigail's eyes twinkled. "You're an adult. You can do what you want. You don't need me telling you how to live your life. I will, however, make sure I'm scarce this evening in case you and Cooper want to ... spend some quality time together."

"On the first date?" Hannah feigned outrage. "That's scandalous, Grandma."

Abigail beamed at her. It had taken time for Hannah to refer to her that way and she was thrilled that the young woman was becoming so comfortable with the word. "You'll be fine."

The television on the nightstand drew both women's attention when the familiar local news music started playing. They were breaking in with a special report.

"What's that?" Hannah asked, leaning forward. "Do you know who that is?"

There was a photograph on the screen, featuring a young woman with blond hair, and the dour newscaster looked grim as he related some tale that Hannah was convinced was of the macabre variety.

"I'll turn up the television." Abigail floated in that direction and showed off her new skills when she hit the button to increase the volume. "I'm getting good, huh?"

Hannah nodded but kept her attention on the screen.

"Holly York is the third woman in the area to go missing from the Bowling Green area in the past month," he said. "All three women are young, in their mid-twenties, and have blond hair and blue eyes. Police haven't indicated whether they believe one person is responsible for the disappearances, but those in the community are starting to worry."

Footage of several women putting up missing-persons signs in an area park filled the screen as the newscaster continued to drone on.

"York was at a local bar on the south side of town two nights ago when she disappeared," he said. "She was out with friends, excused herself to go to the restroom, and never returned. Police were called to the scene within the hour but there was no trace of her, and witnesses could provide no information on her movements. Police are asking that residents — especially women — go nowhere alone after dark until this case is solved. We'll keep you updated with further developments."

"That's sad," Abigail noted as the soap opera they'd been watching before returned to the screen. "I wonder what happened to them."

"I don't know." Hannah shook her head and heaved out a sigh. "Maybe we'll get lucky and find out that they voluntarily took off."

"I doubt it but ... maybe." Abigail's gaze was bright. "Now, what are we going to do with your hair? With that dress, I think you should wear it up. It will make your neck look longer."

"LEAVE THOSE GOATS ALONE, JINX!"

Tyler James, the Casper Creek animal wrangler, shot an exasperated look toward the black Labrador retriever as it bounded around the paddock, excitedly nipping at several young goats as they tried to avoid the dog's attention. When one of the goats, a young black one with a deviant personality, circled behind the dog and gave him a hard charge, Jinx yipped and hopped onto a nearby picnic table to escape.

"I told you," Tyler said wearily, shaking his head. "You've been around those things enough to know that they get vicious."

The look Jinx shot Tyler was one of exasperation. He settled on top of the table and watched as the goat desperately tried to climb the table to mount a second assault.

"What's going on here?" Cooper Wyatt asked as he slid through the fence and surveyed the situation. He looked amused when he saw the way Jinx was cowering on the table. "I thought he and the goats were getting along."

"It goes in spurts," Tyler replied, removing his hat so he could rub at the back of his neck. "One day they'll be fine and the next there will be murder on their minds. You know how it goes."

"I do." Cooper leaned against the fence, taking a moment to smooth down his shirt, and desperately fought the urge to ask Tyler how he looked. "Thanks for watching Jinx tonight so Hannah can leave town for a bit."

Amusement flashed in the depths of Tyler's green eyes. "No problem. What's one more animal? Besides, I have a feeling that you would've wrestled me down and made me eat a pile of hay if I didn't agree."

Cooper was the picture of innocence. "Why would I do that?"

"Because this date is important to you."

"I don't know that I would call it a date," Cooper hedged. He was uncomfortable with the word. It felt too formal, rigid even. That was the last thing he wanted. "It's more of a meal ... with conversation, and maybe a few drinks."

"And just the two of you. How is that not a date?"

"Um ... ." Cooper shifted from one foot to the other, his anxiety kicking up a notch. "Do you think I look okay?" He blurted out the question before he could stop himself. He felt like an absolute ninny for asking it, especially of another male friend, but he had no one else to ask and he was unbelievably nervous.

"I think you look like my cowboy in shining armor," Tyler teased. "I want you to dip me low and kiss me right now, you devilishly handsome man."

The look Cooper shot him was withering. "I'm being serious."

"I know you are, which is why I can't resist messing with you." Tyler's smile stayed in place until he realized Cooper's grimace wasn't budging. "Dude, don't get worked up." He took pity on his friend and clapped his hand on Cooper's shoulder to reassure him. "There's no reason to be nervous. You and Hannah are in sync with one another, to the point where it makes the rest of us uncomfortable sometimes because you look at each other as if you're the only two people in the world."

Cooper let loose an exaggerated sigh. "I know we're in sync. I think that's the problem. What if ... ?" He didn't finish the question. He couldn't.

"What if what?" Tyler prodded gently. "You were going to ask a serious question. I promise to give you a serious answer. That's what friends are for."

Cooper slid him a suspicious glare. "How do I know you're not just going to make fun of me?"

"You don't, but I promise that I'll give you a little break right now because you're wearing your good boots. Things must be serious if you're wearing your good boots."

"How is that not messing with me?" Cooper complained.

Tyler snickered. "Dude, you have got to lighten up. I'm here for you. Tell me what's got you so riled up."

"I just ... what if this is a mistake?" Cooper was desperate enough to lay himself bare. "What if we decide we don't have that spark? Now that we're officially dating, that means we're going to have to officially break up. If that happens, I'm going to have to find another job because it will be too uncomfortable to stay here. I don't want to have to find another job. I like this job."

Tyler had to bite the inside of his cheek to keep from laughing. He'd known Cooper a long time, years upon years, and he'd never seen the man this worked up. To him, that meant Cooper was already too far gone to turn back. He simply didn't see it. "I don't think that's what you're worried about," he said finally.

Cooper's face was blank. "What else would I be worried about? This is a big deal. Technically, she's my boss."

"Which means it might be interesting if she tries to sexually harass you." Tyler sobered when he realized Cooper was in no mood to laugh. "You're going to have to lighten up, man. This is going to blow up in both your faces if you don't unclench just a little.

"As for what I believe you're really worried about, I'm going to tell you," he continued. "You're not worried that the two of you won't fit together. You're worried that you will. Heck, you guys already fit. Now that it's official, though, there's no turning back ... or delaying the inevitable.

"The thing is, I don't think you really want to turn back. You would kick yourself if you screwed this up. You're just excited ... and nervous ... and maybe a little bit of a whiner. Everything is going to be fine." He clapped Cooper's shoulder hard. "You need to suck it up. You've been dying for this date for weeks. It's finally here. Why not just embrace it and have fun?"

"That's easy for you to say." Cooper straightened his shirt for what had to be the fiftieth time. "What if I make an ass of myself? What if I say the wrong thing? What if she decides I'm not as handsome as she originally thought? I know it boggles the mind but women think crazy things sometimes."

Since Tyler recognized the statement for what it was — an attempt at a joke — he laughed, but it was only for form's sake. "You're going to be fine. You and Hannah have essentially been dating since she arrived, although it has been in an informal sense. You've spent the night on her couch, and in her bed." He waggled his eyebrows suggestively, earning a stiff elbow from Cooper. "Not in a filthy way, of course," he coughed out once he'd recovered enough to speak. "You guys have eaten lunch and dinner together every day this week. You've fought demons and witches together. What's the big deal?"

The expression that took over Cooper's face was pained. "I don't want to screw this up."

And there, Tyler realized, was the crux of the matter. Cooper, who never doubted himself no matter what, was afraid to scare Hannah away. He already needed her, to the point where it would break his heart to lose her, but he was just starting to realize that for himself despite the fact that everyone else at Casper Creek had been talking about it for weeks.

"It's going to be okay," Tyler reassured his friend, resting his hand on his shoulder and staring directly into Cooper's frustrated eyes. "You guys are going to have the best date ever. You're going to eat good food, take a romantic walk, and do a little dancing."

Cooper frowned. "We're not going dancing."

Tyler's eyebrows hopped. "How come? Women happen to love dancing."

"Yeah, but ... I'm not a good dancer. I can't do any of those line dances or anything."

Tyler snorted. "You don't have to take her line dancing. I'm talking about a bar that plays power ballads. Women love power ballads. Then all you have to do is take her into your arms and sway back and forth a little, your bodies pressed together." Tyler held out his arm to an invisible partner and showed Cooper what he was suggesting.

Honestly, although he was loath to admit it, Cooper didn't think it was out of the realm of possibility. He liked the idea of holding Hannah close, and even he could sway back and forth in time with the music. Still, he didn't want to commit to that possibility until after dinner.

"We'll see how things go," he said, pushing himself away from the fence and shifting his eyes to the apartment over the saloon. That's where Hannah was waiting for him. "I should probably get going. I don't want to be late."

"Definitely not," Tyler agreed, the twinkle back in his eyes. "Don't worry about Jinx when you bring her back. I'll keep him with me so you guys can have some alone time."

Cooper merely shook his head. "Not on the first date. I'm not an animal."

As if registering what he said, the goat let loose a bleat

and finally managed to get on top of the table, which was enough to send Jinx flying in the opposite direction as he whimpered like an eighty-pound baby.

"Just play it by ear," Tyler suggested, grabbing the goat before it could tear after Jinx. "Let your heart be your guide. You've got this."

Cooper desperately hoped that was true.

TWO

*C*ooper couldn't remember the last time he was so nervous. He'd served overseas, found himself in a bevy of life-and-death situations, and yet the sight of Hannah in the pretty dress was enough to make his mouth run dry and his heart flutter.

"Where are we going?" she asked after securing her seatbelt.

"It's a surprise," Cooper shot her a wink and hoped it came off as flirty rather than deranged. He wasn't the best when it came to flirting. He had a natural charisma but wasn't strategic when using it. People either liked him or they didn't. He was usually fine with that. He wanted Hannah to like him, though.

Of course, she already did. "I like surprises," she beamed ... and then her smile faded. "Actually, I don't like surprises. I'm a little nervous I'm underdressed ... or maybe over-dressed. Am I dressed okay?"

That's when Cooper realized she was as wired as him. He should've noticed it when he picked her up and her hand shook as he gripped it. For some reason, he felt better knowing it.

"You look beautiful." His eyes were keen as they looked her up and down. "You always look beautiful, though. As for the restaurant we're going to, you'll be the prettiest one there ... and not over or underdressed. You'll be perfectly dressed."

The smile she shot him was rueful. "Well ... if you're sure."

"I am." Nervously he reached over the console and rested his hand on top of hers. She didn't pull back. In fact, she turned her hand over so they could link fingers. It was a sweet moment and it made something inside of him ache. Tyler was right, he realized. He wanted this to work out so badly that he was turning himself into a nervous wreck. That's not who he was, nor who he wanted to be. "How was your day today?"

She looked taken aback by the question. "I didn't really do anything today."

"You were upstairs by yourself for a long time."

"Yeah, well ... Abigail." Hannah smiled at the memory of her grandmother practicing her staying power. "She's obsessed with being more visible when she hangs around. She wants to interact with the other workers and even serve as an entertainer for some of the performances."

Cooper cocked his head to the side, surprised. "I ... um ... never really considered that an option. I'm not sure if it's a good or bad thing."

"I think it's a good thing."

"You do?" He arched an eyebrow. "How come?"

"Well, I've been giving it some thought. She wants to feel as if she's part of the town. This place was her life for so long that she can't bear to leave it. If she's involved, she'll be happy ... and there's no reason for her not to be happy."

Cooper slid her a sidelong look. "I think she hung around for more than the town. She hung around for you, too."

Hannah swallowed hard. She was still bitter about never getting to meet Abigail in life. She couldn't help but believe that things would've been massively different for her if she'd been allowed to know her grandmother. As it was, though, Hannah's mother had been estranged from her mother. Then, when she died, Hannah was left with a father who tried really hard but couldn't always summon the emotions Hannah needed. She felt stunted in some ways, but there was no way to go back in time and fix it.

"I like spending time with her," she admitted after a beat. "I just ... it's weird. I never thought I would be hanging out with my dead grandmother's ghost."

"I think it would be weirder to spend time with the ghost of someone who was alive."

She snickered at the joke. "True. It's just ... my life has changed so much."

"Do you have regrets about coming here?" Cooper's heart sank at the prospect.

"No. Not at all." She fervently shook her head. "I know it probably sounds strange, but I felt like this was my home almost from the start. Sure, it was weird. I mean ... I live in a replica of a western town, which just happens to be located on top of a mountain, and I can take a ski lift to work every day if I want but ... it feels like I always belonged here."

"That's not weird." Cooper pulled onto the main highway. "I feel like I belong in this place, too. I'm guessing the pull is different for both of us but it's overwhelming all the same."

"It's definitely overwhelming." She slid her sea-blue eyes to him. "Do you think you'll want to stay here forever?"

Cooper hesitated before answering. He understood what she was asking, what was at the core of it. He knew how he wanted to answer but it seemed a little early in a burgeoning relationship to delve too deep. "I love it here," he said finally. "I don't want to leave. It's hard to answer questions about forever because you never know what might happen, but right now, I can't see myself ever wanting to land anywhere else."

Her smile was serene. "Me either. I just wish they had some shopping close by."

He laughed. "I can take you someplace to shop at some point."

"You don't strike me as much of a shopper."

"Yeah, but I like spending time with you. I think I can take a day or two of shopping if it means we get to spend time together."

Hannah went warm and gooey all over. "Well ... it doesn't have to be right away. Eventually, though, I'm going to need a few things."

"Then we'll make it happen."

"Yeah." She leaned back in her seat, suddenly much more relaxed than she had been. "Where are we going again?"

"I told you it's a surprise."

"I don't like surprises."

"You're going to like this one."

COOPER WAS RIGHT. SHE DID like this surprise. When he parked at a beautiful restaurant on a nearby lake, one that had a balcony that overlooked serene water, she openly gaped.

"Look how beautiful that is," she gasped. The lake looked as if it was on fire thanks to the setting sun. "I didn't even know this was here."

"That's why it's good you have me." He hopped out of the truck and rushed around before she could open her own door and extended a hand to help her down. "I thought maybe we could take a walk around the lake once we're finished. The road that leads through town is right over there." He pointed. "It's cute and quaint."

"Is there shopping?"

He grinned. "And ice cream."

"Who doesn't love that combination?" She was careful as she stepped down, lifting her chin when her chest bumped against his. In the moment, as they stared into each other's eyes, there wasn't another soul in the world. It was just the two of them, oxygen being stolen from their lungs, and sexual chemistry buzzing through the air.

"You look really beautiful tonight," Cooper finally choked out, slipping a stray wisp of hair behind her ear. She'd worn it up, off her shoulders, and he had to keep fighting the urge to rub his hands over the taut muscles. It was too proprietary this early in a relationship. "Have I told you that?"

She nodded, her mind blank. "You look really handsome, too."

"I'm a handsome guy."

The joke had the intended effect and they both laughed, relieving some of the tension.

"You are," she agreed, taking a step back. "This restaurant looks amazing. What do they serve?"

"It's a surprise."

She frowned. "Really? Even the food is a surprise?"

"Every moment with you right now is a surprise," he replied. "Come on." He held out his hand. "I reserved a table on the balcony. You'll be able to look over the menu yourself in a few minutes."

"I guess I don't really have a choice because I'm starving." Her fingers slid through his, a perfect fit. "If I forget to tell you later, this was an absolutely amazing night."

His heart pinged at her earnest expression. "Yeah. It really was."

The hostess was congenial, although the smile she sent

Cooper was of the flirty variety. She was long-legged, brunette, and wearing a dress with a plunging neckline. He barely looked at her because he couldn't look away from Hannah.

"Here are your menus." The hostess kept her smile firmly in place even when she realized Cooper wasn't interested. "Your server will be with you shortly. I hope you enjoy your meal."

"We will," Cooper reassured her, grinning as Hannah eagerly snagged the menu and started looking through it. "What do you think?" he asked her after a few minutes. "Do you approve?"

"It's an amazing menu," she confirmed. "It's really expensive, though." Her eyes were earnest when they locked with his. "You didn't have to go all out like this."

"Why not? It's our first date. I think it deserves to be marked with a special meal."

"Yeah, but ... we've spent time together before this. Any number of those meals we had in my apartment could be considered a date."

"True, but this is official ... and I don't want you worrying about the money. Get whatever you want. It's not as if it's convenient for us to come here on a regular basis. I happen to believe there will be plenty of diner food and tacos in our future. Enjoy this for what it is."

"Okay," Hannah's smile was sunny, to the point of eclipsing the fiery display happening over the water. "In that case, I'll probably get dessert, too."

He chuckled. "Good. I like a woman with a healthy appetite."

"Yes, well ... ." She went back to studying the menu. "What are you going to get?"

"Oh, no," he wagged a finger and made a tsking sound with his tongue. "I don't want you to do that woman thing where I pick something and you make sure to come in with something cheaper. I want you to get what you want."

The problem was, Hannah had no idea what she wanted. She was hungry because she'd gone the better part of the day without eating. She was so nervous about the date she could focus on nothing else. There were so many items to choose from, though, she didn't know what to settle on.

"I was kind of thinking about the prime rib," she admitted after a beat. "I haven't had good prime rib since ... I can't remember."

"They didn't have prime rib in Michigan?" he teased.

"They did, but Michael wasn't a fan of beef. He said it wasn't an elegant meat." She realized her mistake too late to take it back. It was generally considered bad form to mention a previous fiancé on a new date. "I'm sorry. I shouldn't have done that."

He frowned as he lifted his chin. "You're allowed to say whatever you want. I'm not offended because you were with someone before me. I know he was a jerk — and there are things I would like to do to his face with my fists — but I'm not threatened by him. If you belonged with him, you'd still be there. You're not. You're here with me."

Her lips curved in delight. "That was a really good response. Still, I don't want to talk about him. I don't even like thinking about him. I feel like an idiot where he's concerned."

"Why?"

"Because I knew he was bad news practically from the beginning and yet I forced myself to try to hold onto him anyway. I convinced myself I could fix him, change him. That's never possible. You need to find someone who you don't want to change. That's the key."

Intrigue lit his handsome features. "Is there anything you want to change about me?"

The question made her giggle. "I pretty much like you as-is. The only thing I might change is how bossy you are. Since you're the head of security, though, I don't think that would work."

"I guess that means we're going to have to compromise."

"Yeah. I'm fine with compromising." She sipped her water and narrowed her eyes, suddenly suspicious. "Is there something you would change about me?"

"Just one thing."

"What?"

"That thing you do where you ignore advice from the security chief and run headlong into danger. I would appreciate it if you'd stop doing that."

She snickered. "It's kind of funny that our 'one things' play together, huh?"

"Fancy that." He leaned back in his chair, stretching his long legs out in front of him. "I think we're going to be okay, Hannah." He found he was no longer overwrought and nervous. Sitting across from her this way was comfortable, familiar even. "This is going to work out."

His words surprised her, even though she'd been thinking the same thing. "I'm definitely getting the prime rib ... and the garlic mashed potatoes ... and the asparagus."

"You're going to make me suffer through the garlic, huh?" His eyes twinkled. "I guess I could get the garlic mashed potatoes, too. Then neither one of us will even notice."

"That sounds like a plan."

"Yeah. It really does."

THEY WERE BOTH STUFFED AFTER DINNER, and when Cooper brought up walking downtown, Hannah jumped at the chance. So far, she'd seen very little of the area, only visiting one town. This was a new experience for her.

"It's really cute," she noted, her hand in his as they crossed in front of an ice cream shop that had gingerbread trim. "I like it."

"You can't possibly be ready for ice cream. We just ate slices of cheesecake and lava cake that were as big as our heads."

She laughed at the exaggeration. "They weren't that big, although they were really good. As for ice cream, I think I need to digest a little bit before I do anything."

"You and me both." Cooper released her hand and slid his arm around her back. She was slim and lovely, and he adored the way she curled into his side, as if she was always meant to be there. "As for the town, there are other places to eat, too. Like that place right over there." He pointed to a log-cabin-style building with a huge chicken on the roof. "That place may look ridiculous, but the chicken is amazing."

"I like chicken." She snuggled in a little closer to him, absorbing his warmth. "What about the Mexican place?"

"Also good. You've had the Chinese before because I've picked up takeout for us here."

"Really?" She was intrigued, although the bulk of her focus was on his strong jaw. "That's cool."

"Yeah." Slowly, as if feeling her gaze on him, he slid his eyes to her. He wanted to kiss her. It wasn't as if he hadn't already done it ... and more. He was afraid, though. If he started now, he might not stop. They might be arrested for public indecency before the night was over if they weren't careful.

"Um ... ." She cleared her throat, all rational thought fleeing.

"Screw it," he said finally, making up his mind. He leaned down and pressed his lips against hers, sighing as she returned the kiss with enough urgency that he felt his heart begin to pound harder. It took everything he had to pull back at some point, and when he did, her cheeks were flushed and her eyes wide.

"That was ... interesting," she noted.

He laughed at her response. "Yeah, well ... you do things to my head."

"You fuzz up my brain, too," she admitted. "It's kind of nice, though. I've never really had it happen before."

"Me either." He moved his thumb over her brow, marveling at her soft skin. "We should keep walking. If we stand here and stare at each other too long, we're going to draw a crowd."

"Will they think we're performance artists?"

"That or perverts."

His response was enough to elicit a bold laugh from her. "It's a fine line."

"It is. I still want to walk off some of this dinner, though."

"That's probably a good idea." She moved to pull away, but he kept a firm grip on her shoulders.

"We can walk like this."

"Yeah, we can." She slid back into the warm place at his side and they fell into step with one another. They'd spent the bulk of dinner incessantly questioning one another in an attempt to learn things. It was fun enough that she wanted to return to the conversation. "What's your favorite food in the world?"

"Like ... Chinese or Mexican?"

She shook her head. "No. The one food item that you can always eat because you love it. It doesn't have to be fancy. It can be from a fast food restaurant ... or a food cart ... or a Little Debbie box. I just want to know."

"Well, if I'm being honest, I have a weak spot for Taco Bell." He was sheepish. "I know it's not real Mexican food, but those Doritos Locos tacos make me want to sing to the heavens ... while double-fisting the tacos. I don't know what it is, but I eat them at least twice a week."

She laughed, delighted. "That's good to know."

"What's your favorite?"

"Well ... McDonald's has this breakfast sandwich."

"The McGriddle? That's a pretty good sandwich."

She shook her head. "No. Not the McGriddle, although that's really good, too. This is a bagel sandwich, with steak, egg, and cheese. I swear I could eat it for breakfast every morning. I haven't had it since I landed here — I honestly haven't even seen a McDonald's — but I'm going to get one eventually."

He chuckled at her serious expression. "There's a McDonald's not that far from Casper Creek. Now that I know your weakness, I think I have a surefire way to bribe you with food."

"I'm one of those people who can always be bought with food."

"Me, too. I —" He didn't get a chance to finish what he was going to say. The sound of a woman screaming drew his attention to the building down the way. Darkness had fallen while they ate so it took him a moment to register what he was seeing. When he did, he gripped Hannah tighter to him. "What the ... ?"

"Is she going to jump?" Hannah's eyes were wide as she took a determined step forward. "Is that what she's doing?"

Cooper was in the dark as much as Hannah. He took a second to glance around, looking for a group of people to indicate that perhaps this was some stunt gone awry. There was no one, though. Several people were exiting area restaurants, their gazes going to the woman on the roof of what looked to be a bank, but they looked as confused as he felt.

"There is no happiness for those who are lost," the woman announced, moving closer to the edge of the building.

Hannah gripped Cooper's arm tightly. "She's not going to jump, is she?"

He wanted to reassure her that it wasn't a possibility, but the sense of growing dread in his stomach told him otherwise. "I ... ."

"Evil is in the eye of the beholder," the woman announced, extending her arms on either side. "When the devil chases you, the only thing to do is ... fly." With that simple statement, the woman took one more step, and plunged over the side of the building.

"Oh, my ... ." Cooper slid his arms around Hannah's head to hide the view as the woman hit the ground. The noise her body made when making contact with the pavement was disturbing, and he was certain it would haunt his dreams ... and likely Hannah's as well. "Don't look, sweetheart," he admonished as he kept a firm grip on her with one hand while reaching for his phone. "Don't look. You don't need to see this."

Hannah readily agreed, but curiosity was often stronger than common sense. She managed to peek through a gap ... and grimaced when she realized what she was looking at. "Is she dead?"

Cooper nodded. "There's no way she could survive that fall."

"Why did she do it?"

"I have no idea. We need to call someone to figure it out, though. Just hold on. I'm calling Boone right now."

THREE

Cooper kept Hannah tucked in neatly at his side despite the fact that he wanted to take charge of the scene. Even though there were only a handful of witnesses, word apparently spread — and fast — about what had happened in front of the bank. The crowd had easily tripled by the time James Boone arrived to take control.

He was older, in his fifties but still strongly built, and he didn't look happy when he saw the crowd.

"What happened?" He scanned the gathered faces for a familiar one, stopping when he reached Cooper. "I'm talking to you."

"Stay here," Cooper instructed, rubbing his hands up and down Hannah's arms before stepping away. He was loath to leave her, but he had a duty to tell Boone the truth and he wouldn't turn away from that duty.

"She jumped," Cooper replied calmly as he closed the distance. "I didn't see the beginning of it, just the end. We happened to be walking down the street and she started yelling ... and then she just jumped."

Boone cocked his head and studied Hannah's profile. She

remained where Cooper left her, lost in thought, and she didn't make eye contact. "Is she okay?" he asked after a beat.

Cooper shrugged as he glanced back at his date. "It's not easy to see stuff like this. I think she's just in shock ... although not the type of shock that requires a doctor. It happened fast."

"Yeah," Boone heaved out a sigh as his gaze traveled to the roof of the bank. "How did she even get up there?"

"That I can't tell you. She was already up there when we turned the corner. There were a few people watching. You might want to wrangle them up — before they start scattering — and question them. I honestly don't know what to tell you."

"The coroner is on his way," Boone offered. "I have two deputies coming, too. Until then, do you want to stand in and help me ask questions?"

Cooper legitimately felt caught. On any other day, he would've jumped at the chance to help Boone. They were friendly, often hanging out together after work, and Cooper honestly loved the investigative side of things. He wasn't keen on the idea of leaving Hannah, though. "Um ... ."

"You don't want to leave her," Boone surmised quickly. The way Cooper kept looking back at the blonde was an explanation in and of itself. "You know what? This isn't your responsibility. Take her home. Get her away from this."

In truth, that's what Cooper wanted to do. He felt guilty, though, and wasn't sure he should follow through on his instincts. "No." Defiantly, he shook his head. "I'm going to stick with you. I want to help."

"Are you sure?" Boone wasn't convinced. "Maybe that's simply not in the cards tonight."

"It will be fine." Cooper was adamant. "She's okay. I'll stick around until your deputies show up."

"I appreciate it. Just ... give me a second." Boone moved

away from the body and crossed to Hannah. He wanted to see for himself that she was okay. "Hey, Hannah."

She jerked up her head, seemingly surprised at being addressed. "Hello, Sheriff Boone." She forced a smile that was so empty it looked as if it was pasted on the face of a cartoon character. "Nice night, huh?"

He kept his expression neutral as he regarded her. "It is. There's a coffee shop right over there." He inclined his head. "Maybe you should head in that direction and get something to drink, huh?"

The way he phrased the suggestion was enough to snap Hannah out of her doldrums. "I'm fine." She pressed her lips into a line that was more grimace than grin, although appropriate to the situation. "You don't have to worry about me. I've seen things like this before."

Cooper, who had been watching the exchange with a growing sense of dread, made a face. "You've seen people kill themselves?"

She nodded. "In Detroit. There was a suicide contagion a few years ago. For two weeks, it seemed people were jumping off buildings over three counties. I think it was actually only seven people total, but it got a lot of attention on the news. I happened to be near one of the buildings when it happened. I was on my lunch break."

Cooper's stomach rolled at the admission. "I'm sorry that happened to you. Still, you don't have to see this. You can grab some coffee. I'm just helping Boone until his deputies arrive."

Hannah was adamant. "I want to help. I won't interfere. Just ... don't send me away. I don't want to be separated from you guys right now."

There was something so raw about her expression that Cooper couldn't press her. He simply nodded. "Okay. Stick close to me then ... and don't stare at the body. It will give you nightmares."

Hannah had no doubt that nightmares would be on tap regardless. Still, she forced a smile. "Let's do it. I've always fancied myself being an excellent investigator."

"You've got the look," Cooper agreed, winking at her before turning back to Boone. "Where do you want to start?"

"Point me toward someone who was already out here when you arrived."

"Um ... right over there." Cooper aimed his chin at a woman and a man, both of whom looked to be in their late twenties, who stood huddled together near a bench. "They were definitely here. I remember thinking they looked like they were on their first date, too. I don't know why that jumped in my head, though."

"Oh, is this your first date?" Boone smirked as he glanced between a squirming Hannah and Cooper. "For some reason, it feels to me as if you two have been dating for weeks. Maybe that's because you were all over each other from the start. It seems weird that this is your first date."

"Yeah, yeah, yeah." Cooper rolled his neck until it cracked. "Do you want me to act as your sidekick or not?"

"Oh, absolutely." Boone bobbed his head. "Let's talk to the other first-date couple. I'm sure they're just as traumatized as the two of you."

Cooper was morose as he fell into step right behind Boone, making sure to check that Hannah was actually following. Now that she'd had a few moments to collect herself, her color was back and she seemed much stronger. Cooper wanted to ask her about the previous suicide she witnessed but figured now wasn't the time.

"You're okay, right?" he said in a low voice as they traipsed after Boone. "I can take you home right now if you would prefer it."

She shot him an unreadable look. "You don't have to worry about me. I'm stronger than I look."

"Then you must be the Hulk because I've always thought you looked strong."

She was taken aback by the statement. Nobody had ever said anything like that to her. "Oh, well ... I'm sorry. This just isn't how I saw our date going."

He nodded, frustration washing over him. "You and me both. We don't have to stick around forever. Once Boone's deputies get here, we'll head out. I'll get you home."

As if sensing what was really worrying him, Hannah impulsively reached out and grabbed his hand. "It was still the best date I've ever had."

The look in her eyes was enough to warm some of the coldness that had been invading him. "Yeah. It was pretty good."

LEAH WHITMORE AND BOBBY Kane were indeed on their first date. Cooper had pegged that correctly. They met on a website, which Bobby was quick to explain wasn't for desperate people, and had just come from eating Mexican when movement on the bank roof caught their attention.

"At first I thought it was a bird or something," Bobby admitted. He stood close to Leah but didn't hold her hand. He seemed awkward and afraid, which were perfectly reasonable responses to what had happened, Boone silently noted. "I couldn't really see her at first because she was toward the back but ... then she got closer to the lights and I realized it was a person. Even then I didn't think there was anything to worry about ... until she started talking."

"And what did she say?" Boone queried. "I'm told she was yelling. What was she yelling about?"

"It was nonsense really," Leah replied. She didn't look

fearful as much as tired. Apparently this wasn't the sort of first date she had in mind and it showed. She was over the entire situation. "She just kept yelling about things being evil and stopping the evil. There was no rhyme or reason to what she said."

"I can vouch for that," Cooper interjected. "I thought maybe she was doing some weird performance piece or something. She didn't say anything of note, blame the government or anything. She just babbled."

Boone was thoughtful as he stroked his chin. "Did you recognize her? I mean ... are you local?"

Bobby shook his head. "I don't know that I've ever seen her before. It was hard to make out her features when she was on the roof, though, and after ... well, after I didn't look."

"That's understandable." Boone shifted from one foot to the other and then shook his head. "Thank you for your time. You can go now."

Both Leah and Bobby looked relieved at the declaration.

"Thank you." Bobby put his hand to Leah's back and prodded her away from the scene. "Come on. I'll take you home."

"Good." Leah scuffed her feet against the sidewalk. "I can't wait to get out of here."

"I'm guessing you don't want to go out with me again, huh?" Bobby sounded forlorn.

"I wouldn't say that." For the first time, Leah cracked a smile. "I'm picking the spot for our next date, though, and it's going to be someplace without buildings that people can jump off of."

Bobby's grin was sloppy. "Sure. That sounds like a great idea."

COOPER AND HANNAH HUNG AROUND much longer

than they intended. Once the deputies arrived, they found themselves essentially trapped as the witnesses were questioned. Most were caught off guard by what happened and couldn't quite wrap their heads around it. Cooper found that Boone had to ask him clarifying questions more than once, which meant it only made sense for them to stay.

By the time all the witnesses were cut loose, the coroner was on the scene studying the body.

"Looks like crush injuries," he said mildly as he lifted the woman's hand and studied it. "She wasn't homeless or anything. Her dental work is good and her clothes are nice. Somebody should be missing her."

"She looks like one of the missing women I saw on television earlier," Hannah mused.

Boone slid his gaze to her, surprised. "What do you mean?"

"I saw a story on the news when I was freaking out about finding something to wear for our date," Hannah explained. "It was a special report. They said three women had gone missing this month. She looks like one of the photos."

Boone's forehead wrinkled as he looked from the body on the ground to Hannah. When his eyes shifted to Cooper, there was an accusation buried in them.

"Don't look at me," Cooper groused. "I didn't see the report. I can't comment on it."

"I'm not angry," Boone said after a beat. "It's just ... she's right. I don't know why that wasn't the first thing that popped into my head." He knelt next to the body, ignoring the dirty look the coroner sent him for crowding his space. With gentle, glove-covered hands, Boone pushed the woman's hair away from her face and studied her for a long beat. "She does look like one of the missing women."

"Do you know which one?" Cooper queried, his stomach doing a slow roll. It was bad enough when he thought he'd only watched some despondent — or perhaps mentally unstable — woman end her life. The notion that this was somehow bigger, that there was more going on, was almost more than he could stand.

"June Dutton," Boone replied hollowly.

"Are you sure?"

The look Boone shot Cooper was scathing. "I'm sure. I've looked over those photos thirty times. I just didn't think ... I didn't expect ... ." He couldn't finish. It wasn't necessary, though. Both Cooper and Hannah understood what he was saying.

"How did she get here?" Hannah rubbed the back of her neck. "I assumed she was kidnapped, probably murdered. She's not the most recent woman to go missing, though. That woman had the same hair but a different face ... and name. If this woman was alive up until a few minutes ago, where has she been?"

"That's a very good question," Boone noted. "I have no idea ... and she doesn't look as if she's been mistreated. Sure, she's got marks all over her now, but I'm guessing most of those were caused by the fall." He looked to the coroner for confirmation.

"I would agree with the statement, but I can't say that with any degree of certainty until I get her into the lab," the man replied. "It's too soon to tell."

Boone nodded and dragged a frustrated hand through his hair. "She was twenty-seven. In a serious relationship. Loved. How did this happen?"

"I don't know." Sympathy rolling through her, Hannah extended her hand and touched Boone's forearm. "I'm sure you'll figure it out, though."

"I certainly hope so." Boone heaved out a sigh. "Take her home, Coop. She doesn't need to be here any longer. She already saved me a bunch of time. Who knows how long I would've been wandering in circles if she hadn't pointed out the similarity."

"The news report was on right before I left," Hannah offered. "It was still in my head."

"It should've been in mine." Boone shot her a wan smile. "Go on. You and Cooper should get out of here. I'm sorry this ruined your first date. I have no doubt there will be many others to follow, though. You guys are just built that way."

Under different circumstances, Hannah might've been embarrassed by the statement. Instead, she merely smiled. "It was a wonderful date regardless. However, I am sorry about all this. I'm especially sorry for her family. I know you'll figure out what's going on here."

"I certainly hope so."

"I know so."

COOPER DROVE HANNAH HOME AND walked her to her room. It wasn't strictly necessary, of course. He could've dropped her off at the front door of the saloon. That somehow felt incomplete, though, and he wanted to milk every moment he could with her.

"Well, that didn't go exactly how I planned," he admitted ruefully as they faced each other in front of her door. "I'm really sorry."

"You didn't cause this." Her tone was mild and yet still scolding. "Why would you possibly blame yourself?"

"Because, if we'd stuck to the lake for our walk instead of hitting downtown, we could've kept doing what we were doing."

"And what were we doing?" she asked in a teasing manner.

He shrugged. "Getting to know one another. Bonding."

He raised his hand and brushed a strand of hair out of her face. "Pretending there's not a certain crackle in the air when we're around one another."

Heat rushed to her cheeks. "I thought I was the only one who felt the crackle."

"Nope. It's both of us."

"Sometimes it's overwhelming," she admitted.

"It is." He leaned forward until his lips were only inches from hers. "We're still doing this the right way, which means you only get a kiss after the first date."

She giggled at his serious expression, amused beyond belief. "Okay. Just one kiss."

The exchange was soft and sensuous. There was a bit of urgency behind it, but neither pushed past the invisible barrier they'd set up. The inclination was to drag each other to the other side of the door, start ripping off clothes, and fall into bed. It was too soon for that, though. They both realized it. Things were already intense between them. They would only get more intense if they gave in to their urges.

When they finally separated, they both were a little breathless. Hannah giggled lightly as she stared into Cooper's wild eyes.

"That was nice," she said after a beat, internally cringing at how ragged her voice sounded.

"It was *really* nice," Cooper agreed, moving his hand to the back of her neck so he could touch her soft skin. "I had a good time ... despite everything."

"I did, too. As for what happened at the end, you can't blame yourself for that. It's not fair. You didn't do anything."

"No, but I'll always wonder if I could've stopped her. I mean ... if we were only there five minutes sooner, could she have been talked down?"

Hannah thought back to the scene and slowly shook her head. "No. You couldn't have stopped her. I think she was gone from the minute she stepped on that bank roof. I don't know why. I don't know what happened to her in the time she was gone. We can't let it haunt us, though. There was literally nothing we could do."

"Yeah." He let loose a sigh, one that was more about longing than frustration, and briefly pressed his forehead to hers. "Do you want to go out with me again sometime?"

She laughed at his expression. "Yeah. Definitely."

"Good. How about I bring breakfast to the saloon tomorrow and we'll pick a date then. I'm afraid if I don't force myself to leave right now, it's going to be a very different night and we're not there yet."

Hannah wasn't certain she believed that. They felt so in tune at times it was only logical to take the next step. There was no hurry, though. There was no need to rush things. She wanted to embrace the magic of whatever was happening and enjoy it in the proper timeframe. No rushing was required.

"Breakfast sounds great."

"Good." He gave her another kiss, this one soft and quick. "I'll see you in the morning."

"Yeah. You will. I ... ." Whatever she was about to say died on her lips as the distinct sound of nails against hardwood floors assailed her ears. Then, like clockwork, Jinx appeared at the bottom of the stairs. He was so excited to see them, he let out a low woof and started racing up to greet them.

"I'm sorry," Tyler called out, appearing behind the dog. He looked disheveled, and exhausted. "He saw the lights on over here and I couldn't contain him. I tried to wrestle him down, but he's stronger than he looks."

Hannah greeted her dog, the one thing that was absolutely necessary to bring from her old life, with a hug and a series of head strokes as Jinx yipped and placed his paws on her shoulders for a hug.

"Have you been naughty?" Hannah asked on a laugh as Jinx licked her face, and then looked to Cooper for the same greeting. "Have you been getting into trouble?"

"He's been terrorizing the goats, and vice-versa," Tyler replied. "He was fine ... until he realized you were home. I'm really sorry." Tyler pointed his apologetic grimace toward Cooper. "I didn't mean to interrupt you guys."

"It's okay." Cooper forced himself to take a step back. "I was just leaving. I'll see you for breakfast tomorrow, Hannah."

She nodded. "I'm looking forward to it." She opened the door to her apartment to let Jinx inside, lingering a moment to listen as Cooper and Tyler talked on their way out of the saloon.

"Why didn't you make your move?" Tyler complained.

"I did. I don't need a stronger move than that tonight."

"How come? I thought you two would be all over each other."

"We were ... but we don't need to move too fast. Don't worry about it. We're fine."

"If you say so." Tyler sounded dubious. "How was your date otherwise?"

"Eventful."

"Well, since you're not getting any action tonight, you can come over to the barn and tell me about it over a beer or two. I'm dying to hear all the juicy details."

"I don't kiss and tell."

"Oh, please. We both know you want to gossip like a schoolgirl."

Hannah smiled as she shut her apartment door. Despite an unexpected suicide that would likely haunt her dreams, it had been a good night.

FOUR

*H*annah took extra time with her appearance the next morning, something she internally chided herself for even as she was applying mascara. She wanted to look good for Cooper, even though he'd seen her at her absolute worst and didn't seem to care. Still, she wore her favorite pair of jeans — the ones that made her butt look like she belonged in a Beyoncé video — and a blue T-shirt that set off her eyes.

Jinx bounded out of the apartment ahead of her and was already downstairs with Cooper when she arrived. He was stroking the dog, telling him what a good boy he was, when Hannah appeared at the bottom of the stairs.

Silence descended on the saloon as they held each other's gazes and there was a moment Cooper was convinced he might actually stride over to her, take her in his arms, and head right back upstairs. Then he remembered where he was and that he was trying to be respectful and patient.

"Good morning," he said finally, his voice husky. "You look nice today."

Hannah's smile was so wide it took over her entire face. "Have you even looked at my outfit?"

"It doesn't matter." Carefully, he moved around Jinx and stepped in front of her. The way she smiled did something funny to his insides. He couldn't put a name to it, but he liked the feeling. "Good morning." He'd already greeted her, but he couldn't stop himself from doing it again.

On impulse, she rolled up to the balls of her feet and gave him a quick kiss. There was nothing smoldering about it, unlike the night before, but it was familiar ... and sweet. "Good morning." Her grin only widened when she registered the flustered way he looked at her. "What did you bring for breakfast?"

He cleared his throat to force him to return to the here and now. "Eggs. Hash browns. Bacon. The usual."

"Then we should probably eat."

"Yeah." He brushed his fingers over her cheek, held her gaze for a moment longer, and then forced himself to turn back to the table. It felt somehow torturous to look away from her. "I figure a good breakfast is exactly what we need before a full day of tourists."

"Right." Hannah's legs felt shaky as she sat at the table and accepted the takeout container he handed her. "I had a really good time last night. I just wanted you to know that because you seem upset about what happened at the end. That wasn't your fault and it didn't ruin anything."

"It wasn't exactly an uplifting moment, though," Cooper pointed out as he sat next to her. He was determined to keep things light. "Up until then, however, it was a perfect evening."

"It was fun," she agreed, her stomach growling when she opened the lid and got a gander at her breakfast. After the previous evening, she wasn't sure she would have an appetite again. Apparently she didn't have to worry. "I had weird dreams, though."

"Yeah?" Cooper's eyes filled with concern as he handed her strawberry jelly. "Do you want to talk about it?"

"I'm not sure there's anything to talk about. I woke up in the dream and knew it was a dream. You know sometimes how you can do that?"

He nodded. "It doesn't happen to me very often," he noted. "When it does, it's always weird. I mean ... I know it's a dream, but I still react as if it's happening in the real world."

"That's how it was for me. Anyway, I was in a town ... although it wasn't Casper Creek. It wasn't where we were last night either. I'm pretty sure it was a made-up town because there was no rhyme or reason to the layout."

"How so?"

"There were no streets. It was just buildings plopped everywhere."

"Ah. Yeah. Even the oldest towns had roads."

"I was looking around, but it was really foggy. I could hear people talking but not see them and when I called out the only response I got was crying."

Instinctively, Cooper moved his hand to her back and lightly rubbed. It was a way to offer her solace, soothe her. He wasn't sure she realized it, but she needed soothing. That was the reason she brought up the dream in the first place.

"It was like being trapped in a horror movie," she continued. "You know how I told you I like horror movies, right? Well, this was like that and I kept feeling as if someone was following me through the fog, as if someone was stalking me, but whenever I would turn there would be no one there."

"Who did you expect?" Cooper was genuinely curious. "I mean ... were you expecting a Freddy Krueger type? You said you knew it was a dream so that might make sense."

"The only good film in that series was the first. Well, and *Freddy Vs. Jason* was fun. I wouldn't call it good, though."

Cooper made a face. "You really are a fan of the genre. I thought maybe you were just talking about classics."

"Oh, no. I love them all. Good movies. Bad movies. Terrible movies that are so bad they're good. The only thing I don't like is bad movies that don't realize they're bad. Those are the worst."

He pursed his lips in an effort to keep from smiling. The moment seemed to call for some gravitas. He couldn't stop himself, though. "What movie is so bad it's good?"

"Um ... there are like a million of them, including *Bait*, which is a shark movie where killer sharks get trapped in an underground mall after a tsunami and all the shoppers are food."

Cooper's mouth dropped open. "That can't be a real movie."

"It is and it's awesome. I'll show it to you one night. Like ... maybe we can have a movie night or something." She lowered her eyes quickly. "I mean ... if you want."

He rubbed her back even harder. "I want to have movie nights with you. I also want to watch the shark movie where they're in the mall. I've never heard anything more ridiculous so now I have to see it."

She laughed, mightily relieved. "Good. Just so you know, though, I love shark movies ... and monster movies ... and even giant crocodile movies. *Lake Placid* is one of my favorites."

"We'll talk about your taste in movies later," he teased. "Go back to the dream. Did anyone ever come for you in it? Did you have to run?"

"No. That was the most disturbing part. It was just me and the fog ... and the crying I could hear in the background.

I tried to find the source of the crying but there was nothing. It was a little disturbing, though."

"It sounds disturbing." He kept rubbing for a moment and then leaned forward to brush his lips against her cheek. "I'm sorry you didn't sleep well."

"I didn't sleep badly," she insisted. "That wasn't the only dream I had either. It was just the last dream, so it stuck with me."

His eyes lit with intrigue. "What other dream did you have?"

Pink climbed her cheeks. "Oh, well ... ."

"Was I the star?"

"You might've made an appearance," she hedged. "This bacon is really good." As if to prove her point, she tore into it with gusto, making Cooper laugh. He felt like he was in high school again because everything was shiny and new.

"Next time I want a featured role."

The sound of someone — a female someone — clearing a throat at the door caused both of them to jerk their heads in that direction. Becky Gibbons, one of the local witches who was helping Hannah ease into her powers, stood in the opening. Her expression was less than welcoming.

"Good morning," Hannah offered quickly, recovering to the best of her ability. "You're here early."

"My car is in the shop so I had to take a bus and I didn't want to risk being late," Becky replied primly as she headed toward the coffee pot on top of the bar. All the workers knew there was a fresh pot brewing at any time of the day. "I'm diligent about my work."

Hannah pressed her lips together to hide her amusement. Becky was becoming something of a thorn in her side. She was twenty-three, blond, perky ... and always staring at Cooper. She had a crush on him, to the point where it was becoming uncomfortable. When the young woman found out that Cooper and Hannah were pursuing a relationship, she turned overtly hostile with Hannah. She was still docile and flirty with Cooper, but her efforts had started to make him uncomfortable.

"You're a very diligent worker," Hannah agreed, briefly flicking her eyes to Cooper. A strong current of dislike was emanating from him, but she was determined to fix things with Becky before they got worse ... if that was even possible. "What did you do last night? Anything fun?"

Becky rolled her eyes at the question. She didn't even try to hide her reaction. Still, she answered ... and after a few seconds, it became apparent why she answered. "I'm taking a dance class. It's supposed to be for weight loss. Even though my doctor says I'm in the perfect range for my height, I want to get toned and firm." She moved closer to the table, her eyes on Cooper. "It shouldn't take me too long and then I'll be practically perfect."

Despite being agitated with the young woman, Hannah also felt profoundly sorry for her. She was desperate to get Cooper's attention and blamed Hannah for "stealing" him. The thing is, as Cooper had made abundantly clear, it wouldn't have mattered if Hannah never took over Casper Creek. He simply wasn't interested in Becky.

"That sounds fun," Hannah supplied, choosing her words carefully. "I've always wanted to take a dance class, but I have negative rhythm and can't follow simple steps. I tried when I was a kid and the instructor told my mother I was hopeless."

"How long did the dance classes last?" Cooper asked as he mashed his eggs and hash browns together.

"Two weeks."

"That's giving up early."

"Yes, but I'm one of those people who doesn't want to do something unless I can be good at it. I knew I was never going to be a good dancer. So, instead, I joined the newspaper at the school and did much better."

"So you only like doing things you excel at," Cooper noted. "Good to know."

"And yet she's still here," Becky muttered loud enough for everybody to hear.

Cooper slowly sent a dark look in her direction, which she promptly ignored. Instead, she moved to the open chair on his right and slid into it.

"What did you do last night?" she asked. It was clear the question was directed solely at Cooper so Hannah focused on her breakfast.

"Hannah and I went out to dinner," Cooper replied without hesitation. He saw no reason to lie. Becky was going to have to get used to the situation. She was part of the coven at Casper Creek, and although Hannah was still a novice witch, he had no doubt she would eventually take it over. While Becky was a passable witch, she had nowhere near the power that Hannah possessed. They were going to have to come to a meeting of the minds ... or one of them was going to have to go. Since Hannah owned the town, there was only one person who could easily be lifted out of the scenario and banished. He hadn't yet broached the subject with Hannah, but it was only a matter of time if Becky didn't calm herself.

"You ... went out to dinner." Becky licked her lips and glanced between them, her gaze darkening when it landed on Hannah. "I didn't realize you were doing that. Going to dinner, I mean. I thought you were just hanging out here occasionally."

"No. We're doing it all." Cooper was blasé as he turned his full attention back to Hannah. "Are you working in the saloon again today?"

She scowled and nodded as she dunked her toast in an egg yolk. "Yeah. I really want to learn to do something else. I mean ... I don't mind the saloon. The uniform makes me feel a little ... on display."

Cooper's lips curved at the mention of her uniform. It was low cut, which meant that Hannah's assets were on full display when she was slinging drinks. He would be lying if he said he wasn't a fan of the outfit. "I happen to like the uniform."

"That's because you're a dude."

"Yeah, well ... ." His gaze drifted to the swinging doors when he heard steps on the wooden floors. He wasn't surprised to find Boone entering their domain. He often stopped by to chat ... or talk about his newest case. He was a regular fixture at Casper Creek. "Good morning."

Boone merely grunted in response and headed straight for the coffee pot. Becky was busy glaring at Hannah, to the point where Hannah had to put up an invisible wall so she could pretend it wasn't happening.

"You don't look good," Hannah noted. "How late were you on the scene last night?"

"Late enough to confirm you were right," he replied. "It was June Dutton. She'd been gone for more than a week. No one had seen her since then."

"And now she's dead," Cooper mused.

"Who is June Dutton?" Becky asked, confused.

"One of the missing women," Hannah replied. "The ones they're talking about on television. She showed up out of the blue last night and jumped off the roof of a bank. We were there and saw everything."

"On your date?" Becky challenged on a scowl.

Hannah ignored her. "Have you notified her next of kin? That's got to be rough."

"I notified her parents over the phone," Boone replied. "They're not local. She has a boyfriend who works here. He's my next stop."

"That's awful." Hannah made a tsking sound with her tongue. "Did they give you any idea why she might've done what she did?"

"No." Boone shook his head. "They said she was a bright, happy, and bubbly girl. They don't understand how this could've happened. They're basically wrecked."

"That's just ... terrible." Hannah heaved out a sigh. "Where do you have to go to talk to the boyfriend?"

"I just told you he works here."

Hannah, who had just shoveled a huge forkful of hash browns into her mouth, swallowed hard. "I thought you meant he was a local guy. You mean he works here? At Casper Creek?"

Boone nodded. "That's why I stopped in here first." His attention was fixed on Cooper now. "I was hoping you would go with me to talk to him. I expect it to be an emotional interview. You know him."

"Who are we talking about?" Cooper asked, wiping the corners of his mouth. He'd largely lost his appetite over the course of the conversation.

"Jon Dillane."

Cooper stilled, surprised. He wasn't sure how to respond.

"Who is Jon Dillane?" Hannah asked finally. She was still getting to know the workers at Casper Creek and that was a name she didn't recognize.

"He's one of the trick riders," Cooper answered, rubbing his forehead. "Young guy. In his twenties. He's pretty enthusiastic and serious about what he does."

"He's kind of an idiot," Becky countered. "He loves this place."

"I don't see why that makes him an idiot," Hannah countered. "I happen to love this place, too."

"As do I," Cooper agreed, his tone cool. "Jon is a nice guy. I didn't realize he was dating one of the missing women, though. He took two days off last week. I guess we know why."

Hannah couldn't ever remember meeting the individual in question and it made her feel guilty. "Do you want me to go with you when you inform him?"

Boone shook his head and patted her shoulder. Now that he had coffee in his system, he was perkier and could read Hannah's tense body language. "That's not necessary," he reassured her. "This is something I have to do. I want Cooper with me because he knows the guy and I think he'll be a soothing presence. It's not necessary for you to be part of it."

"Because I'm not a soothing presence?"

Boone's lips curved down. "I feel as if I walked right into that one."

Cooper snorted. "You kind of did. Don't worry about Jon, though. I'll go with you. Are we thinking he doesn't know what happened yet?"

"I'm not sure. The only reason I know he was even part of her life was because he was all over her phone ... and I read some of their texts. He was worried sick when she disappeared and he begged her to text him back. She never did, even though she had her phone on her when she died."

"The phone survived the fall?" Cooper queried, surprised. "That was a lucky break."

"It was all because of the way she fell." Boone took another sip of his coffee. "Finish your breakfast. I would like to get this over with now rather than drag it out. I don't want him to find out from someone else."

"You're right." Cooper put his focus on his remaining breakfast. There wasn't much left. "I just wish I'd known Jon was going through something. I would've tried to help."

"Maybe he didn't want to make his problems someone else's problems."

"Probably."

The only sounds in the saloon for the next two minutes were those of chewing. When Hannah glanced up, she found Becky watching her with evil eyes. After that, she avoided looking at the woman. The atmosphere in the saloon was so uncomfortable that Hannah welcomed the sound of additional footsteps, especially when she realized it was Tyler coming through the door.

"Hey," she beamed at him. "I'm sorry. I should've told Cooper to get you breakfast. I didn't even think about it."

Tyler waved off the apology. "It's fine. I have another issue, though. One of my goats is missing."

Jinx, who had been sprawled out on the floor, raised his head. It almost looked as if he understood what Tyler was saying.

"One of the little jerks that likes to terrorize Jinx?" Cooper asked on a smile.

Tyler nodded, although he didn't return the grin. "I don't know how he got out of the paddock. He's gone, though, and I need to find him. I was hoping you could help."

Cooper felt caught. "I have to help Boone with something first. It's important. I can help you after."

"I guess that will work." Tyler looked morose. Even though he complained about the goats, he loved them. It was his adoration of animals that propelled him into this business. "I'm going to head out myself and at least try to find him. I'm afraid, if he wandered too far away, a predator might've got him."

Hannah's stomach did an uncomfortable roll. "I don't start my shift for another few hours," she offered. "I'll help you look. We can take Jinx. If the goat is out there, Jinx will likely be able to find him ... even if he is afraid of them."

"Actually, that's a good idea." Tyler brightened considerably. "Thanks for your help."

"Don't mention it." Hannah ate the last of her breakfast

and turned to Cooper. "Thanks for the food. I ... um ... guess I'll see you later."

Cooper grinned at her uncertainty. "You'll definitely see me later."

"Maybe for lunch."

"Three meals in a row? I think that sounds just crazy enough to work."

Becky scowled. "I'm going to head over to the dry goods store and get set up for the day. I think I've had about all of this that I can take."

Cooper didn't as much as glance in her direction. His gaze was firmly fixed on Hannah. "Be careful when you're out looking for the goat. There are snakes out there ... and other things."

"I can take care of myself," she reminded him.

"I know, but maybe I like taking care of you. Have you ever considered that?"

She went warm all over. "I'll be careful. You do the same. I think your job is going to be harder than mine."

Cooper sobered at the thought. "Yeah. We should probably head out." He wiped his mouth with a napkin. "I'm not looking forward to this, but it has to be done."

Boone was grim. "Then let's do it."

FIVE

*J*on Dillane was a friendly and affable guy under normal circumstances, all smiles and hearty guffaws. He looked worried when Boone and Cooper approached him, however, and the sense of dread that Cooper had been carrying around since the previous evening expanded exponentially.

"Hey," Jon straightened when he saw who was approaching. "Do you have information on June?"

Boone nodded solemnly. "I do. You're the one who filed the missing-person's report on her, correct?"

"Yes." Jon's voice was unnaturally low, as if he already knew what was coming. "You found her, didn't you?"

"We did." Boone licked his lips and prepared himself. It was best to just throw the information out there, like ripping off a bandage. It was the kindest thing. "I regret to inform you that June Dutton died last night after jumping from the Lennox Savings and Loan building. I'm sorry for your loss."

Jon stood there for an extended beat, blinking but silent. Finally, all of the oxygen whooshed out of his lungs. "I don't understand."

Sensing that the man's knees might go out from under him, Cooper moved closer and grabbed Jon by the arm, directing him toward the bench a few feet away. "Sit down," he prodded, being careful not to grip him too tightly. "Get your breath."

Jon let himself be led to the bench and when he sat, it was with a heavy grunt. He looked exhausted, as if he'd been up for a week straight, and the fatigue that was lining his face had yet to give way to grief. "I thought you were going to tell me that she'd been found in a field or something, discarded like trash. I don't understand what you're saying to me."

Boone was gentle as he addressed him. "We're not sure what happened. We just know that at some point, after nine o'clock last evening, she found her way onto the roof of the bank. She then yelled nonsense that nobody understood, about good and evil, and jumped to her death."

"But ... no." Jon vehemently shook his head, as if he were trapped in a nightmare and could somehow dislodge himself if he was determined enough. "June wouldn't kill herself. She was a happy person. She ... was a good person."

"I'm not saying she wasn't." This wasn't the first time Boone had to deliver similar news, and he knew that remaining calm was the most important thing. "We need some information from you."

"From me?" Jon's eyebrows practically flew off his forehead. "Are you trying to blame me for this?"

"Absolutely not." Cooper was firm as he drew Jon's fatigued eyes to him. "We know you weren't there. The thing is ... I was."

"You were there?" Jon's confusion only grew. "I don't understand what you're saying to me. None of this makes sense. Absolutely none of it."

"I didn't realize she was your girlfriend until a few minutes ago," Cooper explained. He wasn't a police officer, but he'd delivered more than his fair share of bad news during his time in the military. Much like Boone, he was well-trained and knew when to take things slow. This was one of those times. "I was at the restaurant at the lake for dinner. Then I went for a walk downtown. I heard her yelling, although I had no idea who she was at the time."

"What did she say?" Jon's voice cracked. "Did she ask for help? I mean ... none of this makes sense. Where was she for the last week? Why did she just up and disappear out of nowhere?"

"We're trying to figure that out," Boone reassured him. "We're not sure where she was, or what she was doing during her time away. We're trying to untangle this mess, and that's why we need your help."

Jon merely blinked and nodded. He was too raw to do anything else.

"What can you tell me about your relationship with June?" Boone pressed. "When did you meet? How long were you dating? When was the last time you saw her?"

"We were happy," Jon replied, rubbing his hands over the knees of his jeans. "We met about six months ago. She worked as a manager at the grocery store out on the high-way. She started in the meat department but was head of the entire produce department within a few months. She was a hard worker."

Boone nodded kindly. "She sounds like a wonderful woman."

"She was," Jon insisted. "We met when I was shopping one day and then flirted for two weeks. I was nervous about asking her out, but I couldn't stop thinking about her. Have you ever met someone and thought 'she's the one'?"

Cooper nodded. That's how he felt about Hannah, although it was way too early to admit that. "Sometimes things just fit."

"They do." Jon's voice was getting stronger. "I asked her out and our first date was a total disaster. I took her to a sushi restaurant and she hates fish. We laughed about it hard after the fact, but I assumed I blew it that night. She went out with me again, though."

"So, you were casually dating?" Boone queried.

"At first. I'd say we went out once or twice a week for a few weeks and then we started going out like four times a week. Then we were seeing each other every single day. We also talked and texted. We were ... in love."

Cooper swallowed the lump in his throat. He was surprised when he felt it, but Jon's earnest nature and obvious heartbreak were enough to get to him. "I'm so sorry. Tell me about her disappearance."

"It was eight ... no, nine days ago now. She left my place in the morning. She was supposed to meet some girlfriends after work for an exercise class. I know she made it to that because I messaged her friends. After that, though, she just disappeared. She didn't go home ... or to my place. She never showed back up to work. She was just gone.

"I called the police right away," he continued, his eyes flicking to Boone. "I called that night. They said I needed to wait twenty-four hours." His voice turned brittle. "I knew that something was wrong, but they wouldn't believe me. They thought I was freaking out over nothing, and look where we are now."

Boone didn't take the criticism to heart. Missing-person cases were always tough. "I'm sorry. We started investigating as soon as the twenty-four hours was up. That was as quick as we could intervene."

"I thought it was already too late by then," Jon admitted, rubbing his hand over his cheek and staring blankly at Cooper's boots. "I assumed it was some sort of serial killer or something, especially after that other woman went missing this week. June was the second. I just thought ... maybe I watch too much television."

His eyes cleared and he focused on Cooper. "That's what my mother said. She insisted I watched too much television and that June was probably fine. She said women were flaky and I shouldn't get too worked up over it. If June was willing to walk away that easily, then she wasn't the woman for me.

"I told her to shut up — my own mother — and hung up on her," he continued. "I thought she'd been taken and something horrible happened to her. Now I find out she was wandering around and ... doing something else. I don't understand any of this."

He was close to the breaking point. Cooper read that and exchanged a quick look with Boone, who only nodded in silent agreement.

"We're going to figure it out," Cooper promised him. "For now, I think you should head home for the day. I'll make sure they know in the front office. We'll get you home and keep you updated when we have more information. Until then, you need to rest."

Jon's eyes filled with tears. "What am I supposed to do without her?"

Cooper felt helpless in the face of the question. He honestly didn't have an answer. "I don't know. You need to rest, though. That's the first order of business. We'll figure it out from there."

"SO, TELL ME ABOUT YOUR date last night," Tyler prodded as he walked the well-worn trail that led to the river with Hannah and Jinx. The former seemed to be in good spirits despite the upheaval of the morning and the latter was busy chasing butterflies as he happily barked and bounced.

Hannah slid him a sidelong look, amused. "What do you

want to know? I'm not going to get into any of the gushy stuff, just for the record."

"Oh. There was gushy stuff, huh?" He bobbed his head knowingly. "I'm never going to let Cooper live this down. Did he spout poetry? Did he tell you he liked the way the moonlight bounced off your hair?"

Hannah snickered at the suggestion. "He did neither of those things."

"Did he at least open your door for you and hold your hand?"

"He did ... although I'm not sure that he would like that we're talking about this. I'm guessing he would be angry if he knew."

"Oh, he'll get over it." Tyler let loose a lazy hand wave. "Cooper's biggest problem is that he feels he has to be a man, and part of that is not admitting when he's excited or nervous. You should've seen him before your date yesterday. I thought he might faint or something he was so worked up."

Even though she felt guilty for talking about him behind his back, she was intrigued enough about Cooper's state of mind to press Tyler on the issue. "What did he say?"

Tyler's eyes gleamed as he turned back to her. "Oh, you're just as cute as him. You want to know if he's said anything of note about you. That's just so ... adorable."

Instead of smiling, Hannah frowned. "You kind of make us sound like middle-schoolers or something," she complained. "We're adults ... and we went on an adult date."

"One I interrupted when I couldn't keep Jinx in check. I'm sorry about that, by the way. I can't help but wonder if breakfast for you and Cooper would've been an entirely different affair if I'd managed to keep Jinx all night like I promised."

Hannah hesitated before responding. "I think it worked out okay." She wasn't sure she should confide in Tyler. He was Cooper's best friend after all, and it was likely he would share whatever she said. She'd yet to find someone to confide in other than her dead grandmother, though, and she was too excited not to gush. "It was actually pretty great. We're trying not to rush things so Jinx arrived at the exact right time."

"See ... that's adorable." He smoothly evaded the elbow she sent in his direction. He was serious when he started speaking again. "Honestly, I think you guys are doing things the exact right way. You'll know when it's time to take the next step. Even though last night was technically your first date, you've already spent a ton of time together and bonded."

"Yeah. We had a good time. Like ... did you know that his favorite movie of all time is *The Godfather*? I don't think I've even sat through that movie from beginning to end."

"That's a total guy movie," Tyler replied as they labored to climb a hill. It was early in the day, but the heat was already growing. "I don't really get the appeal of *The Godfather* either. I think that I'm missing key reserves of testosterone or something."

Hannah snorted. "I think you're perfect the way you are. Although ... what's your favorite movie?"

"*Mean Girls*."

She waited for him to start laughing, convinced it was a joke. When he didn't, she frowned. "Are you being serious?"

"Yup. I love it. What's your favorite movie?"

"*The Exorcist*."

He stilled and fixed her with a surprised look. "That movie didn't come out until well after you were born."

"No, but my mother loved it and she let me watch it when I was way too young. I had nightmares about vomiting up pea soup for weeks. My father was furious. Still, she loved it ... and I think that's why I love it."

He rubbed his hand over her shoulder. "That's kind of

sweet, the pea soup notwithstanding. I ... ." He broke off when something caught his attention to the east.

Hannah followed his gaze, frowning when she registered the strange lump on the ground. Even Jinx had given up chasing butterflies and was heading in that direction. "Do you think that's the goat?"

Tyler didn't immediately answer, instead taking a moment to scan the horizon to make sure they were alone. When he was certain there was no threat creeping up on them, he let loose a pent-up breath. "I think it's my goat."

He increased his pace and cut through the field, making sure to keep an eye out for snakes. When he arrived at his destination, he found Jinx sitting next to the fallen goat. The dog almost looked mournful.

"What happened to it?" Hannah asked as she appeared at his side. She looked as upset as the dog. "Did a predator get it?"

Tyler was careful when he shifted the dead animal, frowning when he felt the texture of the goat's body. "I don't see any large wounds."

"It didn't just die for no reason."

"No, but ... here." He pointed toward a spot on the back of the goat's neck. "Those look like puncture wounds to me, although they're fairly small."

"You just said you didn't see any wounds," she pointed out.

"I meant like missing limbs or gaping chest wounds." Tyler traced his fingers over the puncture marks and lifted his chin, grim. "He feels lighter than he should."

Hannah had no idea what to make of that. "Meaning?"

"Meaning that I think he's missing a lot of blood ... or maybe all of his blood."

Hannah's stomach rolled at the thought. "So ... you're

saying some sort of creature caught your goat and drank his blood?"

"That would be my guess. I'm going to have to get him back to my office to take a better look but, yeah, I think he was drained."

Hannah made a face. "You're not going to make me help you carry a dead goat, are you?"

He shook his head. "I'm going to carry him. I don't want to linger too long, though. If something took out my goat, that means it's big enough to take out Jinx, too. We should head back."

He was serious enough that Hannah knew better than arguing. "Let's go right now."

COOPER STAYED WITH BOONE LONG ENOUGH to drop by the medical coroner's office. Unlike the assistant they'd been dealing with the night before, Jerome Blankenship — one of the three top pathologists in the state — was on duty today. Boone couldn't help being relieved when he saw him.

"I guess they called you in special, huh?" Boone stuck out his hand by way of greeting. "This is Cooper Wyatt. He heads up security at Casper Creek. He was on the street when she jumped last night and her boyfriend is one of the workers up there so he has a vested interest in the outcome."

Jerome nodded in understanding. If he was uncomfortable talking in front of a civilian, he didn't show it. "The missing women in these parts are cause for concern and the governor wants this one solved as soon as possible. He called for me himself and asked that I come up here when he heard what happened."

"I'm glad you're here," Boone offered. "I'm confused on this one and I'm not quite sure what to do. I assumed we had a predator on the loose when all three women went missing. They're a certain type, after all."

"Type?" Cooper lifted his chin, his interest piqued.

"All women in their late twenties. All blonde and blue-eyed. All slim and fit. All could be described as beautiful."

Cooper's heart constricted. "Like Hannah."

Boone shot him a look. "Don't go getting worked up. We just saw Hannah two hours ago. She's out with Tyler looking for a wayward goat. What could be safer than that?"

Cooper let loose a low chuckle. Boone had a point, although he would never admit it out loud. "It was just an observation."

"Yeah, yeah." Boone waved his hand and focused on Jerome. "What can you tell us?"

"Well, for starters, she has any number of injuries that could've killed her," he replied. "She has a significant head wound, two broken arms, one broken leg, eight broken ribs. The fall was great enough that there was no way she could survive."

"We kind of figured that out ourselves," Boone noted. "Please tell me you have more than that."

"What are you looking for?" Jerome asked reasonably.

"What about toxicology reports? I know the big ones take weeks, but you must've done a rapid result one."

"I did and I can say there were no drugs in her system."

"Well, that's a bummer. I was hoping at least to be able to blame this on drugs."

"When I say no drugs, I mean no drugs," Jerome stressed. "She was on regular birth control and there were no signs of that in her system. No multivitamins. No aspirin ... or Advil ... or cold medicine. She was completely clean."

"Basically you're saying she was so clean it becomes strange," Cooper said.

Jerome nodded. "She'd eaten about two hours before her death. Fried chicken and mashed potatoes."

"Which seems to indicate that things were normal up until right before it happened," Boone mused.

"We don't actually know that," Cooper argued. "We just know that she ate. That's it. She could've been forced to eat for all we know."

"You're convinced she was taken for the week she was missing, aren't you?" Boone queried.

Slowly, Cooper nodded. He'd gone over it in his head during the drive to the coroner's office. "I do. It's the only thing that makes sense. She was out with friends, having a good time, and disappeared in the blink of an eye. Her car was gone. She never returned to her apartment for a change of clothes. She had a good relationship and was in love with her boyfriend. She had a good job. There was no reason for her to voluntarily take off."

"There doesn't always have to be a reason," Boone offered. "She could've simply been masking her feelings."

"I guess but ... that doesn't feel right to me."

"There is one more thing of note," Jerome interjected, drawing their attention to him. "There was a strange compound in her blood, one I haven't been able to identify. I'm sending it to multiple labs to see if I can get any ideas from them."

"What can you tell us about the compound?" Boone asked.

"Nothing yet. There's literally nothing I can tell you because I've never seen it before. I don't know what it does because I'm not even sure what we're dealing with."

"Can we get our own sample of that?" Cooper asked.

Jerome looked taken aback by the question. "For what reason?"

"I have military contacts," he replied honestly. "They might be able to offer some help."

"Oh," Jerome took a moment to think it over and then nodded. "I don't see why not. Right now, it's a mystery ... and it's one that might take more time than any of us are comfortable with to figure out."

"We'll definitely take that sample," Boone agreed. "Until then ... keep at it. I'm not sure where to point myself next, but I think answers are extremely important."

"Especially for those other missing women," Cooper said. "I mean ... if June was kidnapped and held for a week, there's a possibility the others are still alive. Maybe there's some purpose these women are expected to serve."

"I think that's stretching it a bit," Boone groused. "We have no reason to believe this wasn't a straight-up suicide."

"And no reason not to continue to search. We need answers. We don't have them yet. That means we can't shut down any possibility, Cooper added"

"I hate to admit it, but you're right. We'll keep digging because that's all we can do."

SIX

*B*ecky was loitering near the downtown area when Tyler and Hannah returned with the goat. The look on her face when she saw the dead animal was one of confusion.

"Why did you kill it?"

Hannah shot her a withering look. "We didn't kill it." In the end, she helped carry the goat after all, but only because she couldn't shake the feeling that the hills had eyes ... and they were being watched. She was nervous enough to risk touching the goat if it meant they could move faster. "Is Cooper back yet?"

"I thought you would psychically know that since you guys are so in tune with one another," Becky drawled.

Hannah didn't have time for a verbal hair-pulling contest. "When he gets here, send him to Tyler's office right away."

"Oh, now you want both of them?"

Hannah wasn't sure how she was supposed to respond. She couldn't ever remember being in a situation similar to this one and she was feeling frustrated. Thankfully for her, Tyler was not having the same issue.

"They're together, Becky," he snapped. "You've got to suck it up. We need Cooper when he gets back. It's important."

Becky looked taken aback to be talked to in that manner. "Since when are you her cheerleader, too?"

"Since she helped me carry a dead goat back to town and I'm pretty sure something bad happened to it in the hills surrounding the town." Tyler wasn't in the mood for nonsense ... and it showed. "We need Cooper when he comes back."

Becky straightened, perhaps realizing that Tyler meant business. "I'll tell him you're looking for him."

"Great." Tyler and Hannah shifted the goat. "Let's get him to my office so I can take a better look. Maybe there's something I can find under a microscope."

"Come on, Jinx," Hannah ordered, causing the dog to stop chasing a squirrel on the walkway in front of the saloon. "You can play with the other goats in the paddock."

Jinx looked mournful at the prospect but obediently followed his mistress. Becky watched the threesome go for a long time, conflicted. Part of her was still angry at Hannah. She couldn't help believing that something was somehow stolen from her, and Hannah was the thief. The other part was curious. If something out there really did kill the goat, that might mean a fight was on the horizon. If that was the case, it would be another chance for Becky to show off her growing witch skills to Cooper. He might be impressed this time and ... .

The sound of a truck pulling into the parking lot disrupted her reverie. She recognized Cooper's vehicle. For once, she had an excuse to seek him out that wouldn't make her look needy, and she was excited to put it to good use ... after talking to him a few minutes, of course.

"Hey, Coop." Her smile was shy as she approached. "You weren't gone very long."

"I wanted to make sure Jon was settled at home and then Boone and I went to the coroner's office," he replied, distracted. The town wasn't yet bustling with activity and he was annoyed that he was stuck dealing with Becky without an audience. He was convinced she was a problem in the making and intended to talk to Hannah about her. That would obviously have to wait ... for now.

"How is Jon?" Becky feigned sympathy. "I can't imagine being in his situation. I mean ... that's the worst thing ever. Can you imagine having someone you care about go missing? He probably assumed she was dead, but then to find out she'd been alive until the very end and then chose to kill herself? That's the stuff of nightmares."

"Yeah," Cooper rolled his neck and heaved out a sigh. "Are Hannah and Tyler back with the goat?"

The fact that he couldn't talk to her for more than two minutes without inquiring about Hannah was enough to set Becky's teeth on edge. "Did you get any good information from the coroner?" she asked, skirting the question.

"We got more questions," Cooper replied, his eyes clear. "Hannah," he repeated. "Is she back?"

"Does every conversation we have need to revolve around Hannah?" Becky's agitation was on full display. "I know she's the new element in town and men love it when they have something shiny and new to fixate on but ... come on. There's more happening around here than Hannah."

Cooper was officially at the end of his rope. "Listen, I don't know what your deal is. I don't know what you're hoping to accomplish here. I need to see Hannah, though. If you're not going to help me, then I'm simply going to track her down myself. All you're doing is delaying the inevitable ... and pissing me off."

Becky narrowed her eyes. She didn't like his attitude. Not one little bit. She also recognized that he was serious about picking a fight. "She's in the examination room with Tyler," she said finally. "They found the goat ... and it was dead. They seemed worked up about it."

Cooper's eyebrows knit together as he started shaking his head. "Why didn't you tell me that from the start? I mean ... what the hell?" He was frustrated as he started moving toward the barn. "I think we should have a talk about this later, Becky."

She brightened considerably. "You want to head out and have a talk? That's awesome."

"No," he shook his head, firm. "I think we — meaning you, me, and Hannah — should have a talk about whether you can continue out here if you're going to keep putting this attitude on display."

Becky's mouth dropped open as the reality of what he was saying washed over her. "You want to fire me?"

"I don't, no. You're making things far too difficult, though. You can't keep walking around with those wounded puppy eyes. We were never together. We were never going to be together. Your attitude with Hannah is uncalled for. She's your boss now and she doesn't deserve this."

"Why is it that our conversations always revolve around Hannah?" Becky queried bitterly.

"Because you turn them in that direction." Cooper refused to back down. "You have a choice to make. You're going to want to make it soon. The longer you keep this up, the more obvious it becomes that something is going to have to give out here ... and it's not going to be the owner of the business who needs to leave to make things more comfortable."

It was only then that the truth behind the words settled on Becky's shoulders. "I ... um ... ."

"Get it together," Cooper instructed. "That's your only option." He turned away from her and pointed himself toward the barn. This was already a long day and it had barely started. "If Boone shows back up, which I'm not expecting, but it's not out of the question, send him to the barn. Do you understand?"

Even though she'd been jolted, Becky scowled. "I'm not an idiot. I can send him over there."

"That would be great."

COOPER LET HIMSELF INTO THE BARN without announcing himself. He was familiar with the set-up and pointed himself toward voices. Hannah and Tyler were talking in grave tones when he approached.

"I feel really bad," Hannah announced. "I mean ... really bad. This poor goat wasn't doing anything but minding his own business and now he's dead. We have to figure out what did it."

"We do," Tyler agreed. He had a lighted magnifying glass over his eye so he could check out the goat's wounds more closely. "These look like teeth marks ... but no teeth I've ever seen. I'm going to need to get photos. Can you hand me the camera over there?"

"Yeah," Hannah bobbed her head and retrieved the item in question. "This is really horrible."

Cooper watched her for a beat, admiring how serious she was and willing to lend a hand, and then he cleared his throat to make his presence known. Hannah was the only one who looked up because Tyler was focused on his job.

"How did things go on your end?" Hannah asked.

"They were okay." He moved to give her a hug, but she held up her hands to stop him. "I carried a dead goat and haven't washed yet. You might want to hold back."

He shook his head and reached for her again. "I'll risk it." He was happy to wrap his arms around her, if only for a few seconds, and he briefly pressed his eyes shut. When he opened them again, he found Tyler watching with speculative eyes and he slowly released her. "You guys are okay, right?"

Hannah bobbed her head. "We're fine. We weren't injured. It didn't even take us very long to find the goat. Tyler figured he would've headed for the river."

"That's where I've found them when they've escaped before," he volunteered, returning to his work. "They're little escape artists. This one didn't make it all the way down there. At least ... we don't think he did."

Cooper sent Hannah a reassuring hand squeeze before moving closer to Tyler. "What do you have?"

"I don't know." Tyler was as frustrated by that answer as Cooper looked. "It's weird. We were only about a quarter of the way to the river when we found him."

"Which means he was barely out of town," Cooper surmised. "Do you think he left of his own volition or was taken?"

"I'm not sure." That was something else that had been bothering Tyler. "They wander away sometimes, but they usually do it as a group. I've never seen one of them do it by themselves."

"Have you found anything else?"

"Just these." Tyler gestured toward the two puncture wounds on the back of the goat's neck. "He seems to be missing all his blood and he looks to have been bitten."

Something occurred to Hannah and she raised her hand as if she was in school, causing Tyler to smirk and nod. "Go ahead, Hannah," he teased.

"Maybe it's the Chupacabra," she suggested.

Cooper blinked several times in rapid succession before responding. "I'm sorry but ... what?"

She ignored his tone. "Maybe it's the Chupacabra," she

continued. "I mean ... it's a goat sucker, right? Maybe that's what we're dealing with."

"The Chupacabra isn't real, though," Cooper pointed out. "It's a myth, a legend. It's basically a folktale."

"I bet people would've said that about witches ... and demons ... and whatever other paranormal creatures are out there that I don't know about."

Cooper hesitated and then shrugged. "I don't know what we're dealing with. We need to be careful until we figure it out, though. That means Jinx can't run around the town on his own."

Hannah hadn't even considered that. "I'll take him to the saloon with me for my shift this afternoon."

"That's a good idea." Cooper moved his hand to her back to rub at the tension pooling there. "While you're doing that, Tyler is going to take me back out to the scene so I can check it out myself."

"What do you think you're going to find?" Tyler asked.

Cooper shrugged. "I have no idea. I want a chance to look before we completely lose the opportunity, though."

"Okay." Tyler removed the magnifying glass. "There's nothing more I can do here anyway."

"I want you to stay here." Cooper was firm when he saw that Hannah looked to be working up to suggesting something. "There's a new bartender today, right? That's the first step to you being able to do other things. You have to help train him. That's your responsibility."

Hannah let loose a sigh, the sound long and drawn out. She knew he was right. Still, she hated being cut out of the investigation. "You'll keep me updated, right?"

"Always."

"Okay." She was resigned to her fate. "I guess it's time to get into that uniform, even though I hate it."

Cooper's lips quirked. "Every man here feels the exact opposite."

"That's true," Tyler offered. "I'm gay and still can't get enough of you in that outfit."

She rolled her eyes. "You don't have to lay it on so thick. I'm going."

"And we'll update you as soon as we get back," Cooper promised. "I need you to stay here, though. You're safe here with all the tourists and other workers."

"Then I'll stay here. You just need to watch your back. I felt as if someone was watching me out there."

"I'll watch my back." Cooper squeezed her hand before releasing it. "You won't even realize we're gone."

"Oh, I'll know." She forced a smile for his benefit. "I'll be fine, though. I'll probably have barely started my shift by the time you get back."

"Exactly."

HANNAH HADN'T BEEN AT CASPER CREEK all that long, but she was already familiar with the routine at the saloon. She was all smiles when she hit the main floor and saw Rick Solomon behind the counter. He had on his costume and was busy wiping things down before the first rush of tourists arrived for the day.

"Hey, Rick," she grinned as she moved to join him. "How are you today?"

"I'm just fine, Boss." He winked at her. "We got a new shipment of sarsaparilla in, I noticed. That's probably good because we were getting dangerously low. I thought I would head back to the storage room and stock that before we get too busy."

"That's fine." Hannah's gaze was keen as she glanced around the saloon. "Where's the new guy?"

Rick snorted. "You just can't wait to abandon me, can you?"

"No, that's not it," Hannah protested quickly. "It's just ... I want to try out different things and I can't do that if you don't have backup. Let's face it, you do the heavy lifting here anyway. I just help you when things get to be too much."

"You're more help than you think," Rick reassured her. He'd always been a calming force when she was feeling frustrated with her new job. "Still, I get that you want to try other things. Abigail always jumped around from job to job and had a ball. As for the new guy, he's getting his costume from Jackie and he'll be right over."

That was enough to placate Hannah, at least marginally. In addition to being the seamstress for Casper Creek, Jackie Metcalf was also the head witch in the local coven. She'd been teaching Hannah a thing or two about her new powers, and Hannah was extremely fond of the woman.

"That's good." She blew out a sigh as she flicked her eyes to the clock on the wall. "The first round of tourists shouldn't be here for another hour. The timing is good."

"Yeah." Rick took a moment to look Hannah up and down. "You seem agitated this morning," he said after a beat. "Is everything okay?"

"It is." She sent him a reassuring smile. "It's just been one of those mornings. I helped Tyler look for a missing goat and it turned out to be dead, so it's just been a bummer of a day already."

"That's too bad," Rick tsked. "The goats are always funny, the way they butt each other with their heads and stuff. I hate to see anything happen to an animal. It makes it somehow worse."

"It does," Hannah agreed. "That's why we're keeping Jinx here with us today," she explained. "I don't want him running around when there's a predator out there."

"It will be fine," Rick reassured her. "Jinx is only excitable for the first few minutes and then he crashes out for the afternoon. He won't be a problem."

"Yeah." Hannah tugged on her bottom lip. She was distracted but knew she needed to focus on her work. "What's the new guy's name again?"

"Nick French," Rick replied. "He's got previous bartending experience so he should be easy to mold."

"I'll worry about that. You take care of the sarsaparilla. We should be ready and raring to go by the time the tourists arrive."

"ARE YOU SURE THIS IS THE SPOT?"

Cooper's gaze was keen as he scanned the ground in the area where Tyler led him.

Tyler nodded, morose. He was feeling sad given what happened to the goat. He couldn't help but blame himself. "Maybe I shouldn't let the goats hang out in the paddock at night."

"You can't blame yourself," Cooper countered, shaking his head as he studied various patches of dirt and grass. "You couldn't have known that this was going to happen."

"No, but he's still gone and those goats are my responsibility." Tyler was adamant. "I mean ... this is really bad. He was a good goat. He was funny with Jinx, liked to terrorize him, and he chased the guests around, too. The kids loved him."

Cooper took pity on his friend. "I know you're attached to all the animals," he started.

"And?" Tyler prodded when he didn't finish.

"And I just realized I have no idea what to say." Cooper turned rueful. "I'm sorry about the goat. I know you think of all the animals as yours. Well, except for Jinx because he's obviously Hannah's dog. You get what I'm saying, though."

"I do," Tyler agreed. "You're saying I can't blame myself for this."

"You can't." Cooper was firm. "This isn't your fault. If we have some sort of predator out here, we need to know it, though." He narrowed his eyes when he caught sight of specific marks in the dirt, frowning as he knelt.

"Do you see something?" Tyler asked, curious. "Do you see paw prints or something? I might be able to identify them if you point me to where to look. I don't see anything."

"They're not paw prints," Cooper said after a beat, his eyes shifting to Tyler's boots. "Are those the same shoes you were wearing when you were out here earlier?"

Tyler nodded, baffled. "Why?"

"Let me see the tracks on the bottom."

Tyler was confused, but he did as his friend asked, lifting up a shoe so he could study the bottom. "Why is this important?"

"Because there are tracks right there," Cooper replied, digging for his phone as he inclined his head. "Someone was in this specific area, and the tracks on your boots don't match the ones right there."

Tyler's forehead wrinkled in concentration. "What about Hannah? I think she had on boots this morning."

"She did, but the tracks are too big to belong to a woman. She has big feet for a woman, but those tracks are still a few inches too large."

"Ah." Tyler bobbed his head in understanding ... and then stilled. "Wait. Are you saying that a human killed my goat? How is that possible?"

"I don't know. I'm going to see if I can photograph these treads, though. Then we're heading back."

"Why?"

"Because Hannah is right. I feel as if someone is watching me out here and it's giving me the creeps."

"What's our next avenue of attack? Where do we look next for clues?"

"I honestly have no idea. I need to think about it. First things first, though." Cooper started snapping photos of the print from various angles. "Once I'm done with this, we'll head back. There's something very weird going on here."

"Was the dead goat your first clue?"

"For today."

SEVEN

*C*ooper was bothered enough by the turn of events that he decided to leave Casper Creek on a mission. He stopped in front of the saloon long enough to check on Hannah, grinning when he saw her explaining how to make drinks to the new guy — a young individual who some might describe as handsome (although Cooper thought the opposite) — and sliding into her role as boss very effectively. The new guy seemed enamored with the way the saloon costume fit her, which was something Cooper wasn't pleased with, but she seemed happy and safe.

That meant he could go on his excursion without guilt, and focus on a different sort of problem … for at least a few hours.

He knew exactly where he was going. He'd been to the small store on the highway so many times he'd lost count. He was grim when he walked inside and fixed the trio of witches sitting at a table with a dark look. "I need to speak to Astra." He didn't stand on preamble. There was no reason. He had things to do, and he was going to do them.

One of the witches, a redhead he didn't recognize, cocked an eyebrow and put her attitude on display. "And who should we tell her is calling?"

Cooper rolled his eyes and fixed his gaze on the witch he did recognize. Garnet Jessup. She was one of Astra's favored sidekicks and had been around for several years. "Tell her I'm here," he instructed. There was no request in his tone, only demand.

Garnet leaned back in her chair, a lazy smile on her face. She didn't appear to be in a hurry to do his bidding. "What makes you think she wants to see you?"

"I don't really care what she wants." Cooper had been in this position numerous times. Astra and her coven of trouble had been responsible for more instances of distress at Casper Creek than he could count. "I'm not playing games, and I don't have a lot of time. I want to talk to her."

"Geez." The brunette witch, also a new face, offered up an exaggerated expression. "You're like no fun, huh? You would think you'd be more fun to hang around with given how hot you are."

Cooper's face remained expressionless. "Get Astra, or I'll just head back and interrupt her myself. I'm guessing that she's up to something in her office — because she always is — and she'd prefer I not see it. Frankly, I'd prefer it, too. Get her and we can avoid that uncomfortable situation, for which you'll be blamed."

Garnet stirred. She recognized the truth in Cooper's words and clearly wasn't comfortable with the prospect of him interrupting the head witch. "I'll get her."

"That would be great. Thanks." He turned to study the paintings on the wall as he waited, doing his best to ignore the other witches. Apparently they were as dumb as they looked because the brunette sidled up to him — even though he had an invisible "do not disturb" sign affixed to his forehead — and offered him a flirty smile.

"I'm new in this area," she announced, as if he should care. "Good for you."

She ignored his tone and pushed forward. "I've only been here two weeks. I'm looking for someone who might be able to show me around the town. You're not perfect, but you are the best specimen I've stumbled across since I arrived in this podunk town, so ... I'm nominating you."

"I would rather brush my teeth with steel wool and gargle with acid." He turned when he heard footsteps on the hardwood floor, his eyes seeking — and finding — the white-haired witch who had been the cause of so much heartache. "Astra. We need to talk."

There had been a time when they were close. Or, well, a time when he thought they were close ... *thought* being the operative word. They dated, spent an inordinate amount of time together, and the entire time she was playing him. He didn't like to think about how she'd managed to bamboozle him — and Abigail in the process — but it was always at the back of his mind. He knew without a shadow of a doubt he didn't have to worry about that with Hannah. She was as direct as they come. Still, though, part of him had trouble trusting.

Thanks to Astra.

"You know my door is always open for you, lover," she teased, her eyes going wicked. "I can't tell you how it warms my heart that you're still willing to visit, keep contact. That tells me you know how this is all going to go."

"I definitely know how it's going to go," Cooper agreed. "You don't seem to realize it, but that's not really my concern, though. I need to know if you've been out on Casper Creek property."

If Astra found the conversational switch jarring, she didn't show it. "Why would you think that?"

"That wasn't an answer."

"You know as well as I do that I've been banned from that property," she said sweetly. "I always follow the rules, and the rules say I can't cross the border."

Cooper snorted and let loose an exaggerated eye roll. "Are you trying to fool them or me? It's not going to work on me, which you know, so that means you're doing it for them. I don't really care what sort of persona you're trying to project these days. There's something going on at Casper Creek, though, and I want to know if you're aware of it."

Even though it was obvious she was annoyed by his tone, Astra was intrigued enough at the prospect of something happening on the land she believed was hers that she cocked her head to the side, considering. "Let's move to the outdoor patio," she said finally. "You can tell me what's going on and I can reassure you that I'm not the reason for it."

"How can you say that when you don't even know what it is? Or so you purport."

"Because I've had other things going on," Astra replied simply, pointing toward her ankle. "I'm just back on my feet after the last time I got involved in Casper Creek business. Surely you haven't forgotten about that so quickly."

Even though he didn't trust her, Cooper felt a small tug of shame. Astra had been involved in an incident at Casper Creek, one where she actually helped Hannah during a demon encounter. She hadn't been evil that day. Er, well, not overtly evil.

"I'm sorry," he said after a beat. "How are you feeling after your fall?"

She snickered at his shift, genuinely amused. "I'm fine. Come on. I have some fresh iced tea in the refrigerator. We can drink and talk."

"Don't bother with the iced tea for me," he supplied. "We both know I'm not going to drink anything you supply."

"Because you're worried I'll poison you?"

Honestly, that wasn't Cooper's chief concern. Giving voice to his real fear wasn't wise under these circumstances. "I'm not thirsty. Let's just do this."

"Sure. I just love the way you talk to me. It's always so respectful."

"I stopped respecting you when you turned on Abigail."

"There are two sides to every story."

"I know all I need to know about this particular story. Let's go."

HANNAH FOUND NICK FRENCH FUNNY. He was young, in his mid-twenties, and he had a lot of gregarious energy. He was always "on," which meant he was cracking jokes at every turn and going out of his way to make her laugh. She figured most of that was nerves. He would settle down eventually. Since she was relatively new herself, she understood about the nerves.

"Did you really dress up like a clown to scare your friends?" she asked as she mixed a gin and tonic. She preferred the easy drinks. When she had to look up the harder ones on the Rolodex she felt like a bit of an idiot.

"I did." Nick was solemn. "One of them still hasn't forgiven me. To this day, when we're at a festival as a group and there's a clown making balloon animals, she crosses herself and insists we go to church to repent for our sins."

Hannah smirked. "Catholic, huh?"

"According to my mother. That's the church I was raised in."

She chuckled and shook her head. "Well, mothers are like that. Just make her happy as long as you can. You'll find that, once she's gone, you'll miss her making you miserable."

Nick shot her an appraising look but didn't question her further. Instead, he shifted his eyes to Rick as he returned from the storage room. "I'm not quite up to Tom Cruise's standards in *Cocktail*, but I'm making great strides."

Amusement lit Rick's features. "Aren't you a little young to be referencing that movie?"

"You would think but there's only so many movies about bartenders and I felt the need to bone up on my pop culture trivia before taking this job. That film happens to be a masterpiece."

Hannah snorted. "That film is all kinds of wrong, but it boasts some great music."

Nick extended a finger. "That we can agree on." He fell silent for a few moments, his eyes traveling to the empty saloon. "Is it normal to have lulls like this?"

Hannah nodded, happy he was asking questions she could actually answer. "Yeah. It's kind of nice. The tourists come up in waves so we basically have three or four solid waves a day and then a little breathing room to clean up and do it all over again."

"It is kind of nice," Nick agreed. "I thought maybe things would be slower than normal because of those missing women. I've noticed whenever a story like that hits people tend to stick closer to home."

Hannah, uncomfortable with the subject, shifted from one foot to the other. "Yeah, well ... it's a little distressing. One of the women has been found, though. She jumped off the top of the bank last night."

"Really?" Nick's eyebrows practically flew off his forehead. "I didn't hear that."

"I don't know if it's made the news cycle that the dead woman is one of the missing," Hannah admitted. "The only reason I know so much about it is because Cooper and I were there."

Rick, his eyes keen, shifted to face Hannah. "You were there? You saw her kill herself?"

Hannah nodded, rubbing her forehead wearily. "Yeah. It was horrible."

"Did she splatter all over?" Nick asked. He must've realized his mistake too late because he quickly raised his hands in capitulation. "Not that I'm gross and want to hear the details about that. I've just seen a lot of movies."

Hannah could see that. He'd dropped more pop culture references in the last two hours than she thought humanly possible. "I don't really want to talk about it."

"Of course." Nick backed off immediately. "I'm sorry if I sounded a little bit excited there. I'm not a ghoul. It's just ... that's like the only thing going on around here right now."

"Yeah. It's scary," Hannah agreed.

They worked in amiable silence for a good thirty seconds, and then Rick was the first to break it.

"I knew her," he announced out of nowhere. "The dead woman. June. I heard it was her this morning when people started talking because Cooper was going to have a conversation with Jon. I couldn't believe it when the news broke."

Hannah flicked her eyes to him. "You knew her? She worked at the local grocery store, right? Is that where you met her?"

"I met her at a bar downtown. We dated for a bit."

The admission threw Hannah off guard. "Oh, I ... didn't know that." Suddenly, she was distinctly uncomfortable. "I'm sorry for whatever she meant to you."

He lifted his eyes and there was no emotion there. "Oh, she didn't mean anything to me. She dumped me right before she started dating Jon. I've always suspected she was cheating on me. I'm not going to miss her."

Hannah swallowed hard and risked a glance at Nick, who looked as uncomfortable as she felt. The conversation had quickly gone off the rails and she wasn't sure how to get it back. "Well, it's still sad," she said finally. "Um ... I guess we should get back to work. The next wave of tourists is due in five minutes."

Rick's smile was back as he regarded her. "I'm looking forward to serving with you."

Hannah couldn't return the words. She no longer felt as if she could look forward to doing anything with Rick.

COOPER MADE HIMSELF AS COMFORTABLE as possible on the patio. Astra had been busy, cleaning the area and improving it so it was actually a delightful space. That didn't mean he wanted to hang around any longer than necessary.

"I see you have some new witches to corrupt," he offered as she settled across from him. "The brunette is a real piece of work."

"Stormy," Astra volunteered. "She just moved here from Montana. Her manners need a bit of improvement. She's not too bad, though."

"I don't like her."

"Who do you like?"

"I like people. I simply don't like the people you seem to surround yourself with."

"Right. You like people." Astra's gaze darkened. "How is your new toy? Hannah, right? That's her name. What a stupid name."

"You know her name." Cooper wasn't in the mood for games. He especially didn't want the conversation lingering on Hannah for too long. In Astra's mind, Hannah was the one who stood between her and what she wanted: Casper Creek. Astra had been convinced Abigail would leave her the property upon her death. She was still smarting from her new reality, specifically the part where Hannah had started manifesting powers that were on par with, if not greater, than the ones Astra possessed.

"She saved your life," Cooper reminded her. "If it hadn't been for Hannah, you would've died in that cave with the demon."

"It turned out the demon wasn't anything to fear," Astra tossed back. "It was the boy Hannah tried so hard to protect who was the problem. Last time I checked, his body was still in that cave. How long are you going to let that situation linger?"

"Not much longer."

"You're just waiting to make sure he's decomposed enough to make an autopsy difficult," Astra surmised. "That's smart. Explaining that the boy was evil won't go over well with local law enforcement, even if Boone is on your side and covers for you."

"I'm not here to talk about that situation." Cooper was firm. "I want to know if you've been up to Casper Creek playing with the goats."

Astra's expression signified she found the question absurd. "Why would I care about the goats?"

He shrugged. "I don't know. One is dead, though. It was killed on the hill by the river ... and it was completely drained of blood."

Instead of bristling at the accusation, Astra pursed her lips, intrigued. "Someone drained all the goat's blood? That's ... interesting."

"I'm guessing the blood was needed for some sort of ritual."

"A witch ritual, right?"

He held his hands out and kept his face impassive. "It's a possibility, isn't it?"

"I hate to break it to you, but if I needed blood for a spell, I wouldn't steal one of Tyler's animals to supply it. That's a risk that I wouldn't need to absorb when there are so many other animals, the sort that wouldn't be missed, running around the countryside."

Cooper had to admit that what she said made sense ... even if it didn't leave him with any comfortable options. "Tyler says there are weird puncture wounds on the back of the goat's neck, like perhaps an animal attacked. Do you know of any such animal in these parts?"

She shook her head, thoughtful. "Not that I'm aware of. I can do some research, although I don't know what good it will do. I ... ." She stiffened when a shadow fell over the table and shifted to look at the open doorway that led back into the store. "Do you need something, Stormy?"

If the brunette witch was concerned about being caught listening, she didn't show it. Instead, she graced the duo with a mischievous smile. "I was just eavesdropping."

"Of course you were." Astra didn't look pleased. "This conversation has nothing to do with you."

"No? I guess not. I thought for sure you were talking about those missing women, including the one who took the header off the bank roof last night. I guess I was wrong."

Cooper shifted in his chair, pinning the woman with a dark look. "How do you know about the woman jumping from the bank?"

"It's on the news."

"It's on the news that a woman killed herself," he argued. "The connection to the missing women hasn't been publicly acknowledged."

"Oh, well, perhaps I just assumed." Stormy's lips quirked as Cooper's eyes narrowed. "I just wanted to remind you that you have a reading in ten minutes, Astra. I can do it if you're otherwise engaged. I'm assuming what you're doing out here is much more ... um, stimulating ... than what you'll be doing inside."

The darkness that crossed Astra's face was enough to cause Cooper to shudder.

"I will handle my clients," Astra countered, her tone biting. "I don't need you to fill in for me. If I ever have need of those services ... well, I'll never have need of those services. We're wrapping up here. I won't be much longer."

"Of course." Stormy bowed low and let loose a giggle before straightening. "Your wish is my command."

Cooper waited until she disappeared back inside to speak. "You realize she's mocking you, right?"

Astra nodded, her eyes still on the doorway. "She's ... spirited."

"She's trouble," he countered. "She's going to be a big, giant headache for you before it's all said and done. You should get rid of her now."

"Get rid of her?" The light returned to Astra's eyes. "Since when are you a fan of murder?"

His stomach rolled at the light way she threw around the word. "That's not what I'm talking about and you know it. I'm not suggesting killing her. I'm saying you should send her away."

"And why would I want to do that when she so obviously makes you uncomfortable?" Astra's expression never changed. "From where I'm sitting, she's an amusing new toy."

"You keep thinking that," Cooper said. "When she stabs you in the back and wreaks havoc on what you're trying to build, you'll feel differently. It will be too late then."

"I can handle my own people."

"I certainly hope so. History says otherwise, though. Unless ... well ... you remember Leanne, right? She was working without your knowledge and tried to kill someone I care about a great deal. I won't sit back and let that happen twice."

"You just worry about your new witch. I'll handle Stormy."

"You'd better. You won't like what happens if you don't."

EIGHT

*H*annah's discomfort with Rick's reaction to June's death didn't ease despite how busy they were with the second wave. She stayed throughout, making sure to help to the best of her ability, and then excused herself during the following lull.

"I'm just going to leave you guys to this for a bit and check on something." She kept a bright smile in place even though she didn't necessarily feel it. "I'll be back in a few minutes."

"Sure." Rick was back to his normal, gregarious self. He didn't act like a man who had been callous in the face of an old lover's death. Instead, he was focused on his job and seemed to get a kick out of Nick's stories.

For his part, if Nick was as bothered as Hannah by what Rick said, he didn't show it. He was back "on," and entertaining anyone who bothered to look in his direction.

"Okay. I'll be back in a little bit." She whistled for Jinx to follow, which he seemed keen to do. The dog gave an excited yip when they hit the outdoors and immediately made a beeline for Tyler's paddock. Since she didn't really have a destination in mind when she left, she decided to follow. Basically, she needed breathing room and Jinx had given her a reason to head in a certain direction. That's all she needed.

Tyler was busy discussing matters of life and death with the goats when they arrived.

"I'm sorry that Billy is gone," he said solemnly to the remaining goats. "I know he was your brother and you loved him, but sometimes things like this happen. I'm sorry for your loss."

Hannah folded her arms over her chest and regarded the animal wrangler with a curious look as Jinx bounded into the paddock and immediately started chasing the goats, who scattered and bleated ... and tried to come up on him from behind to exact revenge. It was like a silly dance, and it never failed to amuse her.

"Are you going to have a funeral for Billy?" she asked, smirking when Tyler turned and fixed her with a rueful look. "What kind of name is Billy for a goat, by the way?"

Tyler shrugged, unbothered by the teasing. "Billy the Kid. In this case a goat kid, but still. It seemed fitting."

Hannah hadn't yet put that together and she laughed when she did. "Oh. I didn't think of that. It's funny. What have you named the others?"

"Wild Bill Hitchkid. Buffalo Kid Cody. Wykid Earp. Oh, and Kid Holliday."

"I sense a theme."

"It seemed fitting given where we are."

"Yeah." She watched him a moment, her heart going out to him. He was doing his best to pretend he was okay, but she could tell the loss of an animal weighed on him. "I'm really sorry." She moved to him and wrapped her arms around his neck, offering a friendly hug. "I know it's hard to lose an animal. When it's Jinx's time — and I'm still in denial that's ever going to happen — I'm going to be a wreck. It's okay to be sad."

"It's okay." He patted her arm. "Jinx still has a lot of years in front of him. As for Billy ... I should be used to this. It's not as if animals haven't died under my watch before. I do the best that I can but there's a circle of life. I just ... it bothers me because he should've been safe in the paddock. I've been all over it and can't figure out how he got out."

Hannah separated from him and planted her hands on her hips as she glanced around. "Well, I can help you look. We'll start from scratch and do it again."

"It feels like a waste of time."

"It's not a waste of time if it makes you feel better."

"True." He pursed his lips as he regarded her. "Shouldn't you be at the saloon? Are you just using my bad mood as a reason to shirk your duties? If so, I applaud you. There's nothing better than playing hooky from work."

"Actually, I just needed a breather," Hannah replied. "Rick is sort of creeping me out."

"Rick?" Tyler's eyebrows hopped. "Why is that? I've always thought of that guy as completely harmless."

"I would've agreed with you until ... um ... did you know that he used to date June?"

"I'm not sure who that is," Tyler hedged.

"The woman who jumped from the bank building last night."

"You mean Jon's girlfriend?"

"Except Rick says that she was his girlfriend first and insinuated that she broke up with him for Jon ... and he didn't seem happy about it."

"Well, no one is happy about being thrown over for another person. I had no idea that Rick was seeing anyone, though. How long ago was this?"

Hannah held out her hands and shrugged. "I'm not

exactly sure. I think Cooper said that Jon and June had been dating about six months, so it had to have been a while ago. He was kind of weird when talking about her death. He almost seemed happy about it."

"Really?" Tyler lifted his chin and glanced back at the saloon. He looked unsettled. "That doesn't sound like him. Are you sure he wasn't joking?"

"I don't really think it's a funny thing, but I'm pretty sure he was serious. Like ... deadly serious. It made me uncomfortable. I wasn't the only one who noticed either. Nick noticed, too, although he got over it a lot more quickly than I did."

"Maybe he realized it was a bad joke. It's not unusual for people to use gallows humor when they're close to a situation. Maybe that's all this is."

"Maybe." Hannah wasn't convinced, but there was no reason to dwell on it ... especially when Tyler had his own problems. She needed to talk to Cooper, she realized. He would tell her if there was anything to worry about. "Have you seen Cooper?"

"He went out with Boone this morning."

"I know, but then he came back and went out with you."

"Right." Tyler internally cringed when he realized the position he'd put himself in. "Um ... have you checked his office?"

Hannah narrowed her eyes. She didn't know Tyler all that well, but the man was an open book. She could tell when he was lying. "You know something."

"I ... why would you say that?"

"Why do you keep answering a question with a question?" Her voice turned shrill. "You're hiding something from me. What is it?"

"I'm not hiding anything from you," he reassured her quickly. "I'm just ... um ... ." In truth, Cooper hadn't come right out and admitted where he was heading once they were finished checking the scene of the goat crime. Tyler knew him well enough to read between the lines, though.

"Tell me." Hannah folded her arms across her chest and adopted a defiant look. "As your boss, I demand you tell me."

Tyler's reaction wasn't exactly what she hoped for. He snorted, shot her a wide grin, and then shook his head. "Oh, you're so cute. No wonder Cooper is head over heels for you. If I played for your team I would fight him for you."

Hannah's mouth dropped open in outrage. "I'm being serious."

"So adorable."

She jutted out her lower lip. "How can I be the boss if nobody respects me?"

"I respect you. I just don't believe you when you throw around the 'I'm the boss' card. You don't have it in you to fire me for not telling you what I know."

"Ha!" She jabbed a finger in his direction, her eyes wild. "I knew you knew something. Talk. You have to tell me."

He hesitated, and then sighed. "I'm going to tell you but only because I wasn't told not to tell you. Actually, I wasn't told anything. This is an assumption on my part. You should be made aware of that."

"What are you assuming?"

"I think — *think!* — that Cooper went to see Astra."

Whatever she was expecting, it wasn't that. Hannah's heart sank. "Cooper is with Astra?"

"He's not with her," Tyler said hurriedly. "He stopped in to see her. At least ... that's what I think."

"Why would he do that?" Hannah's tone was clipped. "I didn't realize they just dropped in to visit one another on a regular basis."

"Oh, geez." Tyler rolled his eyes to the sky, as if pleading with a higher power to swoop down and rescue him. "This is not how I saw my day going. First a dead goat and now this."

"I'm sorry about your goat." Hannah was sincere. "I need to know why you think Cooper is with Astra, though."

"I don't think he's with her. Stop phrasing it that way."

"I'm sorry. How should I phrase it?"

Tyler felt as if he was at the end of his rope. "I think he went to ask her about the goat. Some witch rituals — the darker ones — require the blood of animals. I think he's worried that Astra is playing around on Casper Creek property again."

Realization dawned on Hannah and she felt like an idiot. "Oh."

"Yeah, oh." Tyler's smile was back. "Was that a little bit of the green-eyed monster I saw just now?"

Hannah wished it were that easy to explain. "No. More like the insecurity monster."

"You have nothing to feel insecure about. Cooper likes you. I mean ... he really likes you."

The admission was enough to calm Hannah. Unfortunately, she still felt like an idiot. "I just ... it's hard." She opted to tell the truth. "I really like him, too. Astra, though ... she makes me crazy."

"Astra wants to make you crazy," Tyler pointed out. "Her sole mission is to make you crazy. You realize she wants Cooper back, right? Even if you weren't in the picture, that would never happen. Astra refuses to believe that, though. She thinks you're the obstacle to her happiness.

"The thing is, she'll come after you every chance she gets," he continued. "She believes if she can get you out of the way, she can take back Cooper. That will never happen. He's furious with himself for being taken in by her. He's a little raw when it comes to relationships, too, for the record.

"You mentioned that your ex-fiancé was cheating on you

and said you feel like a moron because you didn't see it. That's how Cooper feels about Astra. He feels like a moron for not seeing what she really was."

"He shouldn't feel that way," Hannah argued. "How was he supposed to know?"

"How were you supposed to know what your fiancé was doing?"

"Because he did it more than once," Hannah replied, not missing a beat. "I caught him and he said he had a sex addiction and I believed him. I'm an actual idiot. Cooper was simply misled."

Tyler stared at her for a long time, debating how he should respond. Finally, he heaved out a sigh. "You believed him when he said he had a sex addiction?"

Hannah's gaze darkened. "Yes, and I don't want to hear another word about it."

"Fair enough." He held up his hands in mock surrender. "I won't ever mention it again."

She held his gaze. "I didn't believe him. I convinced myself he was telling the truth because I was afraid. He was the only thing I knew. It was the only life I knew. I went straight from college to him and I was an absolute idiot for doing it. By that time I was in too deep, though. I couldn't see a way to dig myself out."

"Obviously you did."

"Yeah, but it took way too long and I lost everything in the process. If I hadn't gotten the letter from Abigail's attorney the same day I lost my job, I don't know what I would've done."

"I know." Tyler beamed at her. "You would've not only survived, but thrived. It's who you are. Still, I think things happen for a reason. You were destined to come here. Also, I think you and Cooper were destined to find each other. You don't have to worry about Astra. The only way she'll win is if you let her win."

Hannah sighed. He had a point, although she was loath to admit it. "Don't tell him I freaked out, okay?"

Tyler mimed zipping his lips. "Mum's the word." He smirked and then shifted his eyes to Jackie as the woman crossed in their direction. "Hello, stranger," he called out. "I haven't seen you in days. Are you here to offer your condolences on my fallen goat?"

Jackie's forehead wrinkled. "Your goat died?"

"I guess you're not here for me," he said dryly.

"Which must mean you're here for me," Hannah said on a sigh. "Is this about Becky? She's been a bit of a pill all day. I might've snapped at her a little earlier. I really am trying to maintain my temper with her. She makes it impossible, though."

"This isn't about Becky," Jackie replied, her expression unreadable. "Although, if you're having a problem with her, I can try and handle the situation. Sometimes talking to her is like chatting at a brick wall, but she needs to learn her place."

"I don't think I would phrase it exactly like that," Hannah countered, uncomfortable. "Do you need something?"

"Yeah, and you're not going to like it." Jackie glanced over her shoulder, to where a group of women were standing in the middle of the street. They looked excited, and ready for action ... which was exactly what Hannah wanted to see on new faces in Casper Creek.

"What is it? Do they want to ride a mechanical bull or something? They look like they're geared up for a bachelorette party."

"They are." Jackie made a popping sound with her lips and then pushed forward. "Here's the thing, occasionally — it was rare, but for enough money she would do it — Abigail would allow small overnight parties in the brothel. We're talking bachelorette parties, bachelor parties, and even a few sleepovers for paranormal enthusiasts.

"The rooms in the brothel are all set up for a reason, even though it's not run as a hotel," she continued. "Before she died, those people booked a bachelorette party with Abigail ... and it's tonight."

Hannah felt frozen in place, as if she couldn't find the appropriate words. "W-what?" she said finally.

"Oh, don't make me repeat that." Jackie made a face. "Those women are here for a bachelorette party. I thought they had to be kidding when they arrived, but I checked Abigail's old book and they're most definitely in there."

Hannah felt as if she was trapped on a hidden camera show. "Well ... crap. What do we do?"

Jackie's face was dour. "You're the boss. Shouldn't you be making that decision?"

For the second time in less than an hour, Hannah fervently wished for Cooper. He would have an idea on how to handle this. Since he wasn't there, she made up her mind on the spot. "Okay, well, I'm assuming they already paid."

"They gave a down payment four months ago," Jackie replied. "That's only a quarter of the total bill. We need to charge the rest of the bill, but the thing is, food and drinks were included in the package."

"Well ... crap." Hannah rubbed her forehead. "Did they specify what kind of food?"

"Um ... no."

"That's something at least." Hannah blew out a sigh and rolled her neck, her mind working a mile a minute. "We can pick up food in town if we have to. Danielle is still around, but she might not take too kindly to being forced to cook for twelve at the last second."

"You're the boss," Jackie reminded her. "Danielle will do

what she's told. You have the power to order her to make dinner."

"Yeah?" Hannah wasn't convinced that was true. She'd spent some time with Danielle since her arrival and the woman always made her nervous. "Well ... maybe we'll try that." She slid her eyes to Tyler and found encouragement waiting for her there. "What generally happens at these parties?"

"They usually have a bonfire at the pit, eat, drink, and pretend they see ghosts. That's the whole kit and caboodle."

"Okay. I think we can make that happen ... including the ghost. Abigail is running around after all, and she did leave this mess in our laps. I'll track down Danielle and have her start on the menu. As for drinks ... I'll ask Nick if he wants to stay late and pour for them."

"Actually, you don't have to do that," Tyler countered. "I mean ... ask him to stay a few hours, but there are laws about when we have to stop serving alcohol up here. It's not like the rest of the county. We can't serve alcohol after eight o'clock, and I guarantee Abigail laid that out for them."

That was another small break, Hannah reasoned. "Well, then that means they probably brought their own liquor. We just need to supply them with ice after the fact. We'll get them settled — although we should probably check out those rooms to make sure they're clean before we let them up — and go from there."

"I'll distract them with the animals while you check the rooms," Tyler offered. "The goats are always a big crowd pleaser."

Hannah shot him a thankful look. "Great. That will be a lifesaver."

"It's going to be okay," Tyler reassured her. "You know exactly what you're doing. You've got this."

Another glance at the women had Hannah re-thinking

her decision to let them stay. They were young, loud, and laughing so hard she was convinced they were already drunk. "This is going to be a long night, isn't it?"

Jackie nodded without hesitation. "It is, but we've done it before."

"Then we'll figure it out." Hannah plastered a welcoming smile on her face as she started in their direction. "It's a group of women who want to party. How difficult can it be to help them?"

Behind her back, Tyler and Jackie exchanged weighted looks.

"Famous last words," Tyler muttered.

"She'll be fine," Jackie countered. "I mean ... she'll mostly be fine."

"So ... you're worried, too, huh?"

"You have no idea."

NINE

$\mathcal{J}$f the members of the bridal party noticed anything was wrong, they didn't show it. They "oohed" and "aahed" over the animals, paying particular attention to the goats. Then Becky gave them a tour around town — for once she didn't kick up a single iota of trouble — while Danielle put together a menu that made Hannah's mouth salivate and Jackie prepared the rooms. By the time the women circled back, everything was ready ... and they'd become a horde of squealing and cooing women who Hannah realized were going to keep her up the bulk of the night.

"What's going on?" Cooper asked as he appeared next to her on the walkway in front of the saloon. He seemed confused when he realized the town was still bustling with activity.

Hannah slid her eyes to him and did her best to tamp down the momentary surge of hormones that threatened to take her over. "Hey. Where have you been all day?"

"Did you miss me?" He grinned at her.

She nodded without hesitation. "Yeah. It was a stressful day."

He stilled, shifting the bag full of food he carried to his other hand so he could brush a strand of Hannah's hair away from her face. "What's wrong?"

"A few things happened. I want to hear about you first, though. Where were you?" It wasn't a tease, Hannah told herself. Er, well, not exactly. She simply wanted to see if he would tell her the truth. It was important to her that he did.

"Inside." Cooper inclined his head toward the saloon, his eyes briefly returning to the bridal party. "Although ... I need to know what they're doing here. As head of security, they should be down the mountain by now. The chairlift has been shut down for the night. I know because I saw it happening when I drove by."

"Apparently they're a bridal party Abigail booked before her death that we didn't know about. We figured things out on the fly and they seem to be happy. They're staying in the brothel and they brought their own alcohol. Danielle made them food and they're basically going to amuse themselves with ghost stories all night."

Cooper's forehead wrinkled as he hesitated. "I don't know that I think them running around town all night when we've got a blood-sucking fiend on the loose is a good idea. Tyler showed me the teeth marks on that goat and ... well ... I definitely think there's something out there. That means, until we figure it out, I think someone should always be with Jinx when he does his business."

Hannah smiled. The fact that he was worried about her dog warmed her to her very core. "I've already decided that. Tyler says he'll be extra careful during the day when Jinx is over there and he's my responsibility at night."

"*Our* responsibility," Cooper automatically corrected.

Hannah hiked an eyebrow. "You're going to be here all night?"

His cheeks flooded with warmth when he realized what he'd insinuated. "Well ... I'm going to be here part of the night. I'll help you walk him before I tuck both of you in this evening. That's the right thing to do."

"It's the chivalrous thing to do."

His eyes twinkled with amusement. "That, too."

He led her inside and placed the takeout bags on the table. It was Chinese, a personal favorite, and she smiled when she scented the familiar aroma of her preferred dish. "How did you know I would want the bourbon chicken?"

He slid her a sidelong look and laughed. "Because that's what you always want. Okay, occasionally you want the beef with vegetables, but that's only ten percent of the time. The other ninety percent you want this."

"We've only had Chinese like five times since we've met."

"I extrapolated."

"Ah." Hannah was all smiles as she sat. Then she remembered her conversation with Tyler. "You were going to tell me about your day," she hedged. Part of her was worried he would lie to her. If he did, and she knew about it, she was fearful she would never be able to truly trust him and the possibility set her teeth on edge.

"Well, first I went out to where you guys found the goat and discovered a boot print," he replied, opening a small container and placing the Crab Rangoon at the center of things so they could share the appetizer. "The print seems to suggest a man to me ... unless we're talking about a giant of a woman."

"I have large feet," Hannah pointed out. "I wear a size ten shoe. I'm jealous of the women who have dainty and cute feet."

He shifted his eyes under the table, to where Hannah's

feet rested on the ground. She wore tennis shoes even though they ruined the authentic nature of her costume. When you were on your feet all day, though, sometimes comfort was more important than fashion. "I think your feet are cute."

"I think you're just saying that because you believe you have to."

"No. I believe it."

She snorted and shook her head. "What else happened?"

"Well, the location of the dead goat got me to thinking. It's not that far from the river, and Astra keeps showing up at the river."

The fist that had been wrapped around Hannah's chest for the past few hours loosened. "Astra?"

He nodded. "I went to see her. I don't trust her and I know she's still trying to get on this land to wreak havoc. We may have shut down the tunnels she was using — for now — but she will find a way back. I thought maybe she had already done so."

"And?"

"And ... she claims it's not her, and she did have a reasonable argument to the contrary. She pointed out that if she needed an animal for a ritual that it would be dumb to take one of Tyler's — thus tipping us off that she has access to the property — when she could simply wander out into the wild and find one herself."

Hannah broke the corners off one of the Rangoon pieces, thoughtful. "So ... you believe her?"

"I believe that she doesn't have a motive for killing the goat," he corrected. "It doesn't make sense for her to put herself at risk that way. Of course, that doesn't mean one of her new acolytes wouldn't try to test our defenses. She has two of them."

Hannah lifted her chin, intrigued. "Acolytes?"

"Recruits," he corrected. "Ever since I've known her she's been desperate to create her own coven. Even when she was learning under Abigail she dreamed of being powerful enough to cause people to want to follow her."

To Hannah, that was a foreign concept. "I've always wanted people to do the opposite. Look away. Nothing to see here." She breezily waved her hand. "I can't imagine wanting to be the center of someone's world."

"No?" Cooper studied her face for a long beat. "You might want to rethink that. When you find the right person, I think it only makes sense to be the center of that person's world."

Hannah's cheeks burned with a mix of pleasure and embarrassment when she realized what he was saying. "Oh, well … ."

He chuckled at her discomfort. "You'll get used to it." He took a moment to squeeze her hand before releasing it and turning his attention back to his food. "The thing is, I don't know if I really ever believed it was Astra. It would've made things more convenient if it was her. The boot prints, though … they obviously belonged to a man."

"It's possible Astra planted them there," Hannah offered. "I mean, she's smart enough to do that."

"She is. You'll get no argument from me on that front. I just can't see her exposing herself in that manner if she thought she might lose something in the process. She's a strategic thinker, and that would be a boneheaded move."

"Hmm." Hannah shoveled in a mouthful of rice and thoughtfully chewed before swallowing. "You said she had new followers. Maybe one of them did it — somehow managed to cross the wards — and killed the goat because she thought it's what Astra would've wanted."

"I considered that. One of the new ones — Stormy — has a bit of attitude." He said her name as if it made his skin crawl. "There's something about her I don't trust. I can see her coming out here just to cause problems, get a rise out of us."

"Yeah, but that would also put Astra in danger," Hannah pointed out. "She's our first suspect whenever anything goes wrong up here. This Stormy person would have to know that. If she's one of Astra's followers, she should want to protect her ... not put her at risk."

"Normally I would agree with you. This one, though ... well ... there's something different about her. She was pushing Astra's buttons. It's as if she wants to see how far she can push things with everyone. I taunted Astra a bit, mentioned that Stormy was going to be trouble, but she seems determined to keep her around."

Hannah held out her hands and shrugged. "I guess that's Astra's problem."

"It definitely is," he agreed. "I just don't want it to become our problem." He ate for a bit, his eyes never leaving her face. The next time he spoke, it was with a bit of trepidation. "You were agitated earlier. It was about more than the bridal party. Why don't you tell me about it?"

Hannah sighed. She should've known he wouldn't simply forget the way she pressed him. "I was worried you weren't going to tell me you were with Astra," she admitted. She didn't want him lying to her, so that meant she couldn't lie to him. "Tyler told me and I was a little ... annoyed, although I don't know if that's the right word."

"How did Tyler know? I didn't tell him."

"He figured it out and let it slip."

Cooper waited a beat. When she didn't expand, he pressed forward. "And you were upset because you didn't want me seeing Astra?"

"I just ... well ... I'm a little jealous." Hannah turned rueful and lowered her gaze as her cheeks burned under his calm scrutiny. "She's very pretty."

"She's okay. You're beautiful. That shouldn't matter, though. I'm with you because I want to be with you. Astra is a part of my past."

"I know that," Hannah offered hurriedly. "It's just ... ." She couldn't bring herself to finish the sentence. She didn't need to, though. Cooper understood what she was trying to say.

"It's just that your ex-fiancé cheated on you and you're afraid it's going to happen again."

She nodded. "Yeah. I promised I would never put up with another man cheating on me. It's not that I think you would as much as I'm terrified about how I'll react and ... this is stupid." She rubbed her forehead. "You're not the one who cheated on me. I can't hold you responsible for what he did. I'm so sorry. Please forgive me."

"There's nothing to forgive," he reassured her. "You're allowed to have moments of weakness here and there. We haven't known each other for that long. We're still feeling around, trying to figure things out. It's okay."

"It doesn't feel okay. You've been nothing but kind and gentle with me. You've been completely honest. This is my hang-up."

"And mine is that I'm dating another witch and I'm afraid you'll turn out like Astra," Cooper admitted without a trace of guile. "I know in here that you won't because that's simply not who you are." He tapped the spot above his heart. "In extremely rare moments, though, the fear takes hold.

"Now, I know you're not Astra but that doesn't stop me from acting irrationally sometimes," he continued. "Deep down you know I'm not the douchebag you used to be engaged to." On impulse, he reached across the table and snagged her hand. "I won't hurt you, Hannah. That's not what I want. Not ever. I want to protect you."

The rush of words calmed her, elicited a real smile. "I know. Maybe we both have a few issues."

"And maybe we can work them out together."

She beamed at him. "That sounds like a great idea."

THEY ATE THE REST OF THEIR DINNER IN relative peace. Then, once they were finished, they tossed the takeout containers and took Jinx for his nightly walk.

They held hands as they strolled down Main Street and the voices in the brothel were loud, screechy, and apparently filled with joy.

"Oh, you're going to have the best wedding night," one of the women squealed, obviously to the bride. "No, I'm being totally serious. Everyone should be a virgin on their wedding night."

Hannah pulled up short, suddenly leery. This seemed like a private conversation she didn't want to intrude on.

"You have to check on them," Cooper prodded. "It's your job as the boss. Besides, we need to reiterate to them that walking around outside the brothel is not a good idea."

Hannah didn't look thrilled at the prospect. "But ... I don't want to."

He grinned at the adorable way her nose wrinkled. "Life is full of hard choices." He leaned over and gave her a quick kiss, a silent promise that more was to come. "I'll be with you. It's going to be okay."

She let loose a tortured sigh and then nodded. "Okay. Let's do it."

They released hands when they hit the narrow stairway that led to the second floor of the brothel. Hannah felt as if she was invading their space as she climbed the stairs, but she plastered a bright smile on her face as she crested to the second floor and joined the melee.

The women there seemed to be having a great time. They were sprawled around the space, the bride-to-be wearing a cheap veil and holding a glass of what looked to be a sparkling drink, and they were laughing and having a good time. That made Hannah feel as if she were the school headmistress coming up to ruin the fun.

"Hey, guys." She kept the smile in place as she glanced between faces. "I just came up to check that you're having a good time."

"We're definitely having a good time now," one of the bridesmaids said. Hannah was almost certain her name was Jenn, although it hardly mattered. "Did you bring us a stripper? That was so nice of you. We were bummed when we were told there were no strippers allowed."

Hannah pressed her lips together to keep from laughing and slid her gaze to Cooper, who looked distinctly uncomfortable.

"I'm not a stripper," he said upon finding his voice. "I'm the head of security."

"Oh, it's like a sexy cop," one of the other women said. "He's going to take out some cuffs and try to arrest us before ripping off his pants and starting to dance. Although ... he's kind of a specific stripper, isn't he? He's a honky-tonk cop. It's weird."

"I'm not a stripper," Cooper repeated, forcing Hannah to stare at the wall to maintain her composure. "I really am the chief of security. We're just checking on you before calling it a night ... and making sure you remember the ground rules."

The bride, Heather Clarke, jutted out her lower lip as she twirled a strand of her flaxen hair around her finger. "Oh, are you really with security? That's a total bummer. I wanted you to be a stripper, too."

"I'm sorry to disappoint you," Cooper said calmly. "I really am with security. I want you ladies to have a good time, but it's important that you stay up here." His tone was no-

nonsense. "It's not safe to wander outside the building after dark."

"How come?" Jenn asked on a pout. "What could possibly be so terrible that we need to lock ourselves away?"

"Especially when we have you to protect us," another woman piped in.

Cooper remained calm, but Hannah could see a muscle working in his jaw. He was getting agitated.

"There are rattlesnakes in the area surrounding the town." He was firm, although he didn't raise his voice. "They come into town, too. I won't be here. I don't live here. Hannah lives here, but she'll be locked away in her apartment as well."

"Rattlesnakes?" Heather made a face. "I don't like rattlesnakes."

"Then don't go outside," Cooper shot back. "You'll be fine if you stay inside."

"We really do want you to have fun," Hannah stressed. "You can't wander around, though. It's important."

"We won't wander around," Jenn promised, her eyes back on Cooper. "If he's not going to be here, that means there would be no need. We plan on staying up here. You have nothing to worry about."

"That would be nice."

COOPER WALKED HANNAH AND JINX back to the apartment. The dog went tearing inside the unit and Hannah could hear him bouncing on the bed as he got comfortable. Apparently he was ready to go down for the night.

"You didn't need to walk us back," Hannah said on a breathless whisper as she stared into Cooper's eyes. "I mean … we're okay. I'm not afraid." Her heart pounded, her palms were sweaty, and she found she was nervous despite her bold words. Still, she held it together.

He was as much of a wreck as she was, but he didn't show it. His fingers all but trembled as he brushed them against her cheek. "I want to make sure you're okay, locked away for the night. It's not about being afraid."

"Right." She licked her lips. "Um ... do you want to come in?"

"More than anything." His smile was sweet. "I can't, though. I really do want us to take our time. There's no reason to rush things."

"Right."

"I honestly believe that," he pressed. "It's getting harder and harder to ignore that little voice in the back of my head, though."

"I'm pretty sure that's your hormones."

He belted out a laugh and shook his head. "I'm pretty sure you're right. I'm enjoying what we're doing here, though. I don't want to miss out on something because we felt the need to rush to the finish line."

Honestly, Hannah felt the same way. Her hormones were throwing a riot in her chest, though, and she found herself ridiculously distracted by the warmth crawling over her skin. He did the most fascinating things to her.

"No rushing," she said after a beat. "Even though it might be fun."

"It would definitely be fun." He moved closer, his lips barely an inch from hers. "This is fun, too." The kiss he graced her with was explosive, which he wasn't expecting. There wasn't anything soft about it. From the second their mouths touched, it was as if they were overcome by a force they couldn't control and suddenly they were a sweaty and groping mess.

Somehow — and he would wonder about this the entire night — he found the strength to break away from her before they tumbled over the threshold and started ripping at clothes. His breath was ragged as he took a step back, his chest heaving.

There, they eyed each other for a long time ... and then Hannah started laughing. Once she started, she couldn't stop. Before he realized what was happening, Cooper had joined her. Their chuckles echoed throughout the stairwell.

"And that right there is why I can't come in," he said once he'd straightened and collected himself. "If I come in, our hormones are going to throw a party."

"Yeah. I see that." She wiped her hand over her forehead and briefly shut her eyes. "That was ... wow."

"Yeah." He tentatively reached out and ordered her hair.

"If a simple kiss goes that way, what do you think the next step is going to be like?"

Cooper's heart rate picked up a notch at the visuals that played through his mind. "I don't know. We're not going to find out tonight, though."

"You have tremendous willpower."

Which was being tested, he realized. "I'm feeling a little weak on that front right now." He took another step toward the stairwell to increase the distance between them. "Lock your door. I'll bring breakfast in the morning. I ... um ... don't look at me that way."

Hannah's smile was serene. "What way was I looking at you?"

"You know exactly how you were looking at me. I can't take it." He laughed as he slid down three steps. "I'll see you in the morning."

She blew him a kiss and waved. "Sweet dreams."

"I can guarantee my dreams won't be a problem."

TEN

*H*annah's dreams weren't as sexy as she was hoping. Instead, she found herself trapped in the foggy dreamscape again ... and she didn't like it.

"Hello?" she called out in the vain hope she wasn't alone. Again, the only sound she heard was the crying.

"Hello?"

She remained rooted to her spot, her hands clenched into fists at her sides in case she needed to protect herself. She knew it was a dream. There was no doubt in her mind ... and yet she couldn't stop the fear from building in her chest.

"Hello?"

She kept calling out even though no one answered. There was no one there except the source of the crying, and that individual sounded as if she — and Hannah was certain she was dealing with a female — was a great distance away.

Part of her wanted to travel through the mist to find the source of the crying. The other part recognized that could be a dangerous proposition. The dread that filled her at the notion was daunting, and instead of rushing headlong into the fog, Hannah stayed.

"If you talk to me, I'll come to you," she offered. It was the best she could do by way of compromise. "I can't risk it if you don't talk to me. This could all be a trick." Even as she said the words, she hesitated. Was it a trick? Was someone trying to draw her out of her safety zone?

"I won't leave unless you talk to me," she said with as much determination as she could muster. "That's all there is to it. You can't lure me away from this spot without giving me more to go on."

Silence met her demand. She'd just about given up and was going to try to find a way to claw her way out of her dream when she heard it.

Hannah.

It wasn't a voice as much as a whisper on the wind.

She swallowed hard. "Hello?"

Hannah. We're waiting for you. Come to us.

Her heart gave a little jolt at the words. "Who are you?"

Come to us. You must step through the fog to find us.

In her head, Hannah understood that it wasn't a victim speaking. No, whoever was calling to her was dangerous ... and playing a game.

"I think I'm good here," she countered. "In fact ... I'm not leaving this spot." She folded her arms over her chest and stared defiantly into the fog.

You have to come. There's no other choice. If you want to save them, you must cross the barrier.

Them? Hannah squinted and tried to stare through the thick coverage. She couldn't see more than five feet in front of her. After that, the fog was a dense wall ... and it made her increasingly nervous because she'd almost managed to convince herself that she could see ethereal hands reaching through the thick air to grab her.

"I'm not looking for you. I'm not an idiot. I just ... why can't I wake up?"

You're not dreaming. This is real. You must save us.

"No, you're the ones who aren't real." Hannah was adamant. "I won't go out there. You can't make me."

Have it your way then.

Hannah braced herself for an attack, convinced it was coming, and then a real voice broke through the haze. It sounded far away but the more she focused on it, the louder it got.

"Hannah!"

She bolted upright in her bed, her eyes wild and her hair standing on end, and met Abigail's concerned eyes. "What happened?" she rasped out.

Abigail tilted her head to the side, uncertain. "I don't know. You tell me."

"I just ... it was a dream. A really weird dream." Even as she said the words, Hannah wasn't certain they were true. She felt lost, out of her depth ... and completely shaken. "Why were you calling my name?"

As concerned as she was, Abigail couldn't focus on her granddaughter's bad dream. They had other things to deal with. "You have to get up and head over to the brothel."

"The brothel?" Hannah was a slow starter on a normal day. This morning she felt as if she were wading through quicksand. "I don't understand."

"The bridal party." Abigail forced herself to remain patient. "They're waking up ... and one of them is missing."

"Missing? But ... ." Slowly, Hannah's mind began to clear. "One of the members of the bridal party is missing, the ones who were staying in the brothel because you arranged it before your death and nobody knew about it."

Abigail was sheepish. "I'm sorry about that. No, I really am. It slipped my mind, what with the death and all."

Hannah made a face. "That was a lovely guilt trip."

"Thank you." Abigail didn't break stride. "You need to get dressed and head over there. It's urgent."

"Right." Hannah reached for the jeans she'd discarded before climbing into bed the previous evening. "I should call Cooper."

Abigail eagerly bobbed her head. "You should. You don't need to handle this alone. Call him, and then get over there."

"I'm on it. I ... thank you for waking me up." She meant it. She was worried if Abigail hadn't yanked her out of the dream when she did something truly horrible would've happened. "You're getting good at being seen and heard, huh?"

Abigail chuckled hoarsely. "It pays to practice."

"It definitely does."

COOPER ARRIVED ON THE SCENE WITHIN twenty minutes. He was freshly showered and had changed into clean clothes — something Hannah was mildly bitter about — and he was all-business when he arrived.

"What's going on here?"

"I'll tell you what's going on." Jenn, the drunk bridesmaid from the night before, pushed in front of the other terrified women and fixed Cooper with a dark glare. "Heather is missing. You remember Heather, right? The bride. Well, she's missing and I'm going to sue the crap out of you for this."

"Go ahead." Cooper was calm as he switched his gaze to Hannah. She looked frazzled, her blond hair sticking out at odd angles, but otherwise she was unhurt. That was the most important thing. "You signed releases to be allowed to stay here. Those releases have been run through ten lawyers ... and I warned you about wandering around last night. We're not liable for one of your group taking off."

"She didn't take off," Jenn fired back, fury practically dripping from her tongue. "She wouldn't do that. I mean ... why would she? She's marrying the man of her dreams, an investment banker for crying out loud, in two days. She's about to get everything she's ever wanted."

"I'm not saying she voluntarily disappeared," Cooper countered. "Although I can't rule that out. I'm saying that perhaps she wandered out of the room and decided to investigate the town while the rest of you were sleeping. It looked like there was some imbibing going on upstairs last evening."

Jenn's mouth dropped open. "Are you blaming this on us?"

"I'm saying that we need to find her." Cooper was calm. "I'm going to start a search myself. Hannah, I need you to tell any worker who shows up that I need him or her to join me. Okay?"

Hannah dumbly nodded. "I should help."

"No." Cooper vehemently shook his head. "I want you to stay here. You can coordinate things, act as a liaison with the bridal party." He lowered his voice so only she could hear. "Call Boone and ask him to send some men. This will go quicker if we have more bodies."

Hannah hesitated and then asked the obvious question. "Maybe she's in the same spot we found the goat."

He didn't want to entertain that possibility, but he didn't see where they had a lot of choice. "I'm going to check that area myself. I don't want you getting ahead of yourself, though." He moved his hands to her arms and vigorously rubbed. "We don't know what happened. This woman could've panicked last night and decided to run from her wedding. It's a distinct possibility."

Jenn's gaze was withering. "It's not a possibility," she growled. "Did I not tell you she was marrying an investment banker? Do you have any idea what that means?"

"She'll always have a calendar ready?" Hannah asked blankly.

Cooper was mildly impressed that Jenn's head didn't pop off her neck given the amount of steam she was generating. It wasn't a funny situation and yet the red-faced woman's reaction struck him as absolutely hilarious.

"No, you moron," Jenn snapped. "It means she'll be set for life. She had to look long and hard to find a guy who could give her the life she envisioned. She didn't just run off less than forty-eight hours before her wedding. That's not how this works."

Cooper was mildly disgusted at the way the woman was talking — marriage for money was a huge turnoff to him — but he managed to keep the disdain from his face. "I'm going out right now to look for her. What I want from you is cooperation. You need to call her family and see if she's checked in. The same with her fiancé."

Jenn balked. "I can't do that. He'll know she's missing if I call. If he thinks she bolted, he might call off the wedding so he can say he was the one to do it."

"What's more important here?" Cooper challenged. "Is Heather's life or this investment banker's ego the thing I should be most worried about?"

Jenn looked legitimately caught. "I don't know. Can't we worry about both?"

"Geez." Cooper pinched the bridge of his nose and looked to the sky, frustration evident. "Just call everyone you know who might've seen her," he barked. "That's an order, not a request. I'm heading out to start my search. Hannah, call Boone for me and then get cleaned up. We might need you before this is all said and done."

Hannah didn't need to ask for what. She knew what she might be tapped for. She had magic at her fingertips. It might be needed if this wasn't wrapped up smoothly ... and fast.

. . .

HANNAH WAS FEELING BETTER, more on her game, when she returned from her apartment the second time. She'd taken a quick shower, not bothering to dry her hair or apply makeup before joining the growing throng in the middle of the street.

"Anything?" she asked Tyler when she spotted him.

He shook his head, thoughtful. "No, but Boone has arrived with three deputies. They're out helping Cooper right now. The good news is that the spot where Billy died is empty. She's not there."

"How is that good news?" Hannah was genuinely curious. "All that means is that she could be dead somewhere else."

"Oh, are you feeling grumpy today?" Tyler poked her stomach to elicit a smile and was disappointed when she didn't acquiesce. "You shouldn't panic, Hannah. People go missing all the time. They're also found all the time."

"Yeah, but Heather Clarke had blond hair and blue eyes. She was in the right age range and was having a good time with her friends last night. There was no reason for her to voluntarily disappear."

"Are you saying that you think someone lured her out?"

"Just like your goat was lured away. In fact ... ." Hannah trailed off when Arnie Morton, the Casper Creek black-smith, made his way in her direction. He didn't look happy. "Uh-oh."

Tyler followed her gaze and smirked when he saw what had her so worked up. "Calm down. His bark is worse than his bite."

"He's been nothing but nice to me," Hannah countered. "I mean ... absolutely lovely. It's still weird for me to talk to him because I know he was having sex with my grandmother and it freaks me out."

Tyler let loose a hollow laugh. "Ah, the things that traumatize us." He rubbed her shoulder and focused on Arnie. "Hey, old-timer. You're out and about early. You usually don't bother getting up until right before the tourists are due to arrive."

In addition to Tyler and Hannah, Arnie was the lone individual who often spent the night at Casper Creek. He had his own place in town, but he preferred the bedroom he'd built over his shop. Hannah had her suspicions — the biggest being that hanging around the town made him feel closer to Abigail — but she'd never given voice to them out of respect. She wasn't about to break that streak now.

"It's hard to sleep through this," Arnie groused. "What's going on?"

"One of the members of the bridal party went missing," Tyler replied. "They're mounting a search for her."

"Oh, well, I knew it was a mistake having them up here." Arnie's expression was dour. "If you ask me, that was your biggest boneheaded move yet."

Hannah shifted when she realized the statement was pointed at her. "Hey, this wasn't my idea. They just showed up out of the blue yesterday. Abigail is the one who booked this little event ... and then didn't tell us about it."

Arnie's eyes flashed with annoyance. "Oh, well, blame the dead. That's great because she's not here to defend herself."

"Don't worry. I blamed her to her face when she woke me this morning."

Arnie's eyes widened. "She woke you? That means she's getting stronger."

"She is. It's a good thing. The bridal party was not my idea, though, and I'm not taking the blame for it. I did the best I could given the circumstances. There was very little I could do once they arrived with their copies of the signed contracts."

"I guess." Arnie worked his jaw and shook his head. "Still, I think it's a bad idea going forward. I know Abigail got a kick out of it, but it's dangerous. Look what we're dealing with now. We have a missing bridesmaid."

"Actually, we're missing the bride," Hannah countered. "She was there when Cooper and I swung by to check on them before bed. They were a little tipsy but not belligerent. They promised they wouldn't leave. Apparently they didn't keep that promise."

"Oh, I know for a fact they didn't keep that promise," Arnie intoned. "I saw them out and about around midnight last night."

Hannah stilled. "You did? All of them?"

"It wasn't all of them. I ... well ... I think it was only one of them. I remember thinking it was weird. I'd gone to bed about thirty minutes before and was dead to the world. It was the sound of voices that woke me. I was about to go out and yell at them to shut their mouths when I realized one of the voices was male."

Hannah was taken aback. "What? You heard a man out with them? Why didn't you say anything?"

"Because I didn't know it was important," he fired back. "I was trying to sleep — as any smart person would be doing at that hour — and I was confused. Sue me."

Hannah had to bite the inside of her cheek to rein in her temper. "I apologize. I didn't mean to jump all over you. It's just ... it was a bridal party. There were no men. What can you tell me about him?"

"Are you kidding?"

"No."

Arnie shifted his gaze to Tyler. "Is she kidding?"

"Not last time I checked," he replied dryly. "Why are you getting so worked up? Just describe the guy to her so she can tell Cooper. It might be a lead."

"I don't have to describe the guy to her. I know who he is."

Hannah's eyebrows drew together. "You do? Who is it?"

"Rick Solomon."

Hannah's mouth went dry as she struggled to find the right words.

"Are you sure?" Tyler finally asked.

"Of course I'm sure. I'd know that guy anywhere. He's annoying. He never shuts up when I stop into the saloon for a drink. I think I know what he looks like at this point."

"Right." Tyler tracked his eyes back to Hannah. "We need to call Cooper back. He's going to want to hear this."

Hannah's hands were shaking as she reached for her phone. "You don't think ... ?" She left the question hanging.

"I don't know what to think," Tyler replied gently. "Just text Cooper and get him back here. We'll go from there."

COOPER WAS POSITIVELY APOPLECTIC when he arrived.

"Tell me the story again," he insisted, folding his arms and glowering at Arnie.

"I've already told you twice," the older man barked. "It isn't going to change, or get dirty. Well ... any dirtier than it already is."

"Tell me again," Cooper insisted. "I need to know."

"Geez." Arnie threw his hands up in defeat. "I was in my apartment, in bed and dozing. I wasn't quite asleep yet. I was in that twilight area between sleep and wakefulness. Voices outside woke me, so I pushed back the curtain and saw Rick on the street with a woman in a white veil. They were talking and having a good time."

"And you're sure it was Rick, right?"

"Don't ask me that again!" Arnie extended a warning finger. "I know who it was. I'm not an idiot."

"And you didn't think it was weird that Rick was here after hours hanging around with a member of a bridal party?"

"How was I supposed to know that he wasn't supposed to be here?" Arnie snapped. "I thought maybe Hannah was paying him overtime to entertain the women so she wouldn't have to deal with it."

"Except we can't serve liquor after eight. Well, technically we can't sell it. We can drink it ourselves, but that's the limit of it."

"Oh, man." Arnie's expression twisted. "I forgot about that. Abigail was furious when she got the liquor license restrictions. I remember her stomping up and down and complaining about it for days. I can't believe I forgot that."

"I don't understand what he was doing here," Cooper said, his eyes moving to Boone as the sheriff approached. "It doesn't make any sense."

"Anything?" Boone queried.

Cooper caught him up to speed. When he was finished, Boone was grim.

"I don't suppose you know where this guy lives, do you?"

"I can look it up," Hannah volunteered. "It would have to be in his personnel file."

"Do that," Boone instructed. "I'm going to leave my men out here searching, but we've come up completely empty so far. I don't know if that's a good or bad thing."

"As long as we're not stumbling across a body, it's a good thing," Cooper said. "I'll go with you to get the address, Hannah. Then Boone and I will head directly over there."

"You just want to play kissy face with your girlfriend," Boone lamented.

Cooper ignored the jab and slung an arm over Hannah's shoulders as he walked with her. "How are you feeling?"

"I've been better," she replied honestly. "I don't know

what to do. I didn't hear anything outside last night." She thought about the dream, the voices, and her heart gave a long roll. She couldn't bring that up now, though. They had to focus on Heather. "Do you think she's already dead?"

"I honestly don't know. I think it's possible she's dead. I also think it's possible she ran because she realized she didn't want to marry the investment banker. Love is more important than money. Maybe she came to that realization on her own."

"Or maybe the same person who took the other women took her, too," Hannah suggested. "Maybe she's going to end up on the roof of a building in a week and jump to her death."

"Maybe," Cooper conceded. "We don't know anything yet. We need that address and we'll go from there."

ELEVEN

*R*ick didn't answer his door so Boone opened it for him ... using his foot. He went in with his gun drawn, but the apartment was completely empty.

"That was like an episode of *Chicago P.D.*," Cooper commented as he followed the sheriff inside. He was antsy as he looked around, desperate for a clue. The apartment was pristine, though, and there didn't appear to be a thing out of place.

"I called in for the warrant," Boone supplied. "It's been approved, even though we don't have it in physical form. It's on the way. We're cleared to look around."

"Anything off limits?" Cooper asked as he eyed the computer on the table in the kitchen.

"Nope."

"Then I'll start with that." Cooper booted up the computer as Boone prowled around the small space. The apartment wasn't big, five-hundred square feet essentially, and only had one bedroom. While Boone hit the bathroom and bedroom, Cooper navigated the computer. It wasn't password-protected, which was a relief, but the desktop was flooded with folders and he had no idea where to start.

It only took Boone a few minutes to complete his search and he was annoyed when he returned to the kitchen. "There's nothing here. It doesn't even seem like the guy lives here. There are a few items of clothing in the closet, a book on the nightstand, a few pairs of shoes ... and that's it."

Cooper, his gaze intent on the computer, made sympathetic noises. "Keep looking."

"Oh, thank you for the advice," Boone drawled. "I never would've considered that. Oh, wait, I'm the sheriff. That means I give the orders."

"Do you want to go through all the stuff on the computer?" Cooper asked dryly. "If so, I have to warn you, the computer is where he keeps his mess. There is stuff everywhere."

Intrigued, Boone moved behind the security guru and stared at the screen over his shoulder. "What do you have?"

"I'm not even sure. There's a lot of porn, though."

"That doesn't necessarily mean anything," Boone hedged. "I mean ... porn isn't illegal unless it's of underaged girls or really freaky stuff. It's not that sort of porn, is it?"

"No. There is a theme, though." Cooper double-clicked on one of the photos and brought up an image of a naked sexy blonde. She had her hands tied behind her back, a pleading look on her face, and her legs were open so there was absolutely nothing left to the imagination.

"Oh, geez," Boone slapped his hand over his eyes. "I didn't need to see that."

"If it's in my head, it's in your head," Cooper drawled. "He's got at least a hundred images here, and they're all similar."

Boone peeked between his fingers. "All blondes?"

"With blue eyes, at least as far as I can tell."

"Well, that's ... just great." Boone straightened. "That indicates a pattern, although it certainly doesn't prove guilt. Some guys just have a type."

"The bondage is a reoccurring theme. There are cuffs or ropes — mostly ropes — utilized in almost all the photos I've clicked on."

Boone rolled his neck until his eyes landed on the ceiling. "Well, awesome. That still doesn't make him guilty."

"Heather Clarke was blond. Blue eyes, too."

"Yeah, but we don't know that anything has happened to her yet," Boone reminded him. "She could just be on a walk ... or hiding in town at a coffee shop or something. She might've gotten cold feet and decided to run."

"According to her friend, that's impossible. The husband-to-be is an investment banker, which seemed very important to the story."

"That means she's marrying for money. She might've convinced herself she was okay with it and then thought differently while drunk."

"They only brought two vehicles," Cooper pointed out. "Both are still in the lot by the lift. She didn't leave via that route."

"Which is good because that would've meant drunk driving." Boone inhaled through his nose and rubbed the back of his neck, thoughtful. "Maybe she called someone to pick her up. We should check her phone records."

"That's a good idea," Cooper agreed. "How did she leave Casper Creek, though? The ski lift is off during the overnight hours. The building the controls are housed in is locked tight, especially after the demon incident."

"You can get to Casper Creek from the back roads. That's how you get there every single day."

"Most people don't know that, though."

"It's not that hard to figure out when using GPS. She

could've called a friend, freaking out, and had them pick her up behind the saloon."

Cooper tilted his head, considering. "No. That doesn't feel right. Hannah would've woken up if headlights hit the parking lot over there. It's right by her bedroom."

"No. The main bedroom in that apartment looks out on Main Street."

"Hannah won't sleep in that room. She still considers it Abigail's domain."

"Abigail is dead."

"And yet still hanging around." Cooper lifted his eyes and smirked. "Trust me. I've tried talking to her about it, but she's not keen on the idea. I can't make her do something she doesn't want to do. She'll switch over eventually. Until then, she's in the guest room, which looks out on the parking lot."

"She might've been tired," Boone argued. "She had a long day yesterday, what with finding the goat, working a full shift, spending time with you, and dealing with the brides. She could've simply passed out and slept like the dead. It's been known to happen."

"It has." Cooper would never suggest otherwise. "She had Jinx with her, though. He's not always the best guard dog during the day — or even at night when demons break in — but he always barks at cars. I've heard him up there when other people pull into the lot. He would've woken up."

Boone wanted to push back on the statement, but he didn't disagree. He'd seen the oversized dog go after vehicles a time or two himself. "So ... it's unlikely she left via that route."

"Not unless she walked all the way to the road, which is a mile out."

"A mile doesn't feel like much when you're drunk," Boone pointed out. "She could've easily made that walk."

123

"Yeah. You should send some deputies down there to search the area, maybe tap some members of the K-9 unit."

"That call has already been placed," Boone reassured him. "The only true lead we have is Rick ... and I know very little about him. What can you tell me?"

"I looked over his personnel file when I was with Hannah, who is more upset than she lets on, by the way. He's single, lives alone, and basically keeps to himself. There's nothing to know about him."

"Maybe that's the way he wants it."

"Because he's a serial killer?" Cooper lifted his chin. "I might be able to get behind that scenario if it weren't for one thing. June Dutton jumped off that building herself. There's absolutely no doubt about that. I was there. She wasn't pushed."

"That doesn't mean she wasn't coerced. She could've been drugged. The coroner said there was a strange compound in her body. Maybe that compound was a new drug we don't know about."

"One that made her commit suicide?"

Boone held out his hands and shrugged. "Stranger things have happened. There are plenty of drugs out there that alter minds. It might not be that she was trying to kill herself. Maybe she was delusional and thought she could fly or something. Maybe she saw a different scene than you did. We may never know."

"I guess." Cooper wasn't convinced that was possible. "That just doesn't feel right. I know that I have no basis for arguing but ... it's weird. It's so, so weird. She was up there, yelling at the crowd, and she seemed lucid."

"You weren't up close and personal with her, though. You were at the end of the block. Could you really see her face?"

"No. That's a point. I don't know why I'm so bothered by

all of this. I've seen death before. I've seen suicides before. This one, though, it feels so very wrong."

"You're bothered because Hannah was with you and you're so far gone you don't want anything bad to touch her," Boone replied reasonably. "Oh, don't bother denying it. I've seen the way you look at her. It's ridiculous ... and kind of sweet. It's the sort of thing I don't want my daughter to ever bear witness to."

Cooper was baffled. "And why is that?"

"Because it's like a fairy tale. I'm not saying it never happens — obviously it does — but it's not the reality for everyone and I don't want her to get her hopes up."

"Because you don't want her to be happy?"

"Oh, don't be an idiot. Of course I want her to be happy. She's my daughter. I don't want her to dream that particular dream if it's never going to happen, though. If she focuses on getting that, she might lose something equally good ... if not as public. Just because you and Hannah are mushy messes, that doesn't mean everyone has to be that way."

Cooper couldn't contain his eye roll. "We're not mushy messes. We're ... in a new relationship. It's always like this at the start of a new relationship."

"Really? It's never been that way for me. I loved my wife a great deal, but we were more practical. As I recall, it wasn't this way for you and Astra either. Hannah is special."

Cooper scowled at the mention of Astra's name. "Did you have to bring her up?"

"I always like to mess with you."

"Well, don't bring her up." He turned back to the computer. "I need to go through the rest of these files. They're all we've got."

"I'm not going to stand in your way."

.   .   .

CASPER CREEK WAS OPENING FOR business despite the missing bride. The rest of the bridal party departed not long after the police made their presence known. They were distraught, but there was nothing they could do. By the time the K-9 units arrived to start searching the area around the town, the bridesmaids were horrified enough to beat a hasty retreat. That included the demanding Jenn, who finally seemed to understand the reality of the situation.

Cooper texted long enough to tell Hannah that Rick was in the wind. They weren't sure where he was. Since he was scheduled to be at work that afternoon, he warned her to be on the lookout and text him should the man show up. If he did, she was ordered to hide out upstairs until the cavalry arrived. She wasn't keen on the notion but agreed to it simply to avoid an argument.

Despite all that had happened, it was still early. The ski lift would start in two hours, which meant Hannah had time to do ... something. The only problem was, she had no idea what that something should be.

She left Jinx with Tyler when she headed out in the direction of the river. It would've been smarter to take the dog, but she wouldn't risk him for anything and she was leery about the trip. Technically she knew that Cooper and Tyler had already checked the area, but she was antsy enough to double-check ... and maybe use her magic if she got a chance.

Unfortunately for her, the K-9 unit happened to be in that location when she passed, the dog alerting on the very spot where the goat died. She thought about explaining to the deputies what happened but ultimately kept her mouth shut. If they had questions, they would ask Boone. She didn't want to draw attention to herself.

She kept walking past them, as if she had the river as a destination the entire time. She didn't stop until the familiar rushing water started filling her heart and ears and she almost sighed when she landed on the banks, removed her shoes, and plunged her feet into the water.

She was going to have to wait it out. If she wanted to use her magic to search for Heather, she was going to have to pick a time when there was no chance of one of the deputies seeing her. It was better to be safe than sorry.

She was lost in thought, her mind on a million different things, when a voice broke through her reverie and caused her stomach to plunge.

"Oh, well, fancy meeting you here ... again."

Hannah didn't have to look up to know who was speaking to her. "Astra." She was grim when she lifted her chin, internally groaning when she caught sight of the white-haired witch. Even though the woman would be considered odd-looking by a great many people, Hannah was always wistful when she saw her. She found Astra beautiful, even if she was convinced the woman was evil and should be avoided at all costs. "What are you doing out here?"

"I happen to enjoy the river as much as the next person," Astra replied airily. "I don't believe it's against the law for me to be out here. Since the boundary to your property ends on that side of the water, that means I'm well within my rights to enjoy the serenity of this place." She kicked off her shoes, bunched her skirt, and slid her feet into the water. The expression on her face practically dared Hannah to pick a fight with her.

Since she was tired, and a little bit heartsick over what happened to Heather, Hannah saw no reason to turn the quiet afternoon into a witchfest.

"I don't care where you decided to commune with nature."

"No?" Astra popped her lips and grinned. "That's a bit of a disappointment." She was silent for a beat. "Where is your bodyguard? You usually don't go anywhere without him."

"I left him back with Tyler. Given what happened to the goat — which I know you're aware of — I didn't want to risk him."

For a brief moment, Astra looked confused. Then she laughed. "I wasn't talking about the dog, although I do miss him. He's the best thing about you. I was talking about Cooper. You two seem joined at the hip these days."

"Oh. He's with Boone. We had an incident at Casper Creek this morning."

"Another one? You guys are turning into a real hotbed of activity. What happened today?"

Before Hannah had a chance to answer, a shadow detached from a tree about twenty feet down. There, a beautiful brunette in shorts and a T-shirt cleared her throat to get some attention ... and then proceeded to laugh. "You should pay more attention to what's going on with your neighbors, Astra," she chided, moving closer. "What's happening down there is big news. It's going to cause a panic throughout the entire area before the day is out."

Hannah narrowed her eyes. "Who are ... ?" She ultimately didn't need to ask the question so she regrouped. "You're Stormy, aren't you?"

Stormy beamed at the question. "I see my reputation precedes me."

"I don't think it's a good reputation, so I wouldn't get too excited." Hannah flicked her eyes to Astra. "Cooper mentioned her."

"I'm sure he did." Astra made a face. "He's the chatty sort ... at least with you. When he stops by to talk to me, it's because he wants to accuse me of something."

"If it's any consolation, I don't believe he really thought you were responsible for the goat. That seems like a silly thing to be worried about in light of what's going down now."

"Which is?"

"A woman is missing," Stormy supplied. "She was staying at the brothel last night with a group of her bridesmaids — she's supposed to be getting married the day after tomorrow, but that won't be happening — and she got up and went for a walk in the middle of the night. Nobody can find her."

Suspicion lit Hannah's face as she slowly slid her eyes to Stormy. "How can you possibly know that?"

"Everybody is talking about it."

"But ... they're not. It just happened. So far, only a few of Boone's deputies have been called out to the scene. They're purposely trying to keep it under wraps because they don't want to start a panic in the community."

"I think it's a little late for that." Stormy laughed jovially as she dipped her toes in the river. "Wow. That is cold. How can you stand it?"

"It's comforting," Astra shot back, her narrowed eyes focused on Stormy. Hannah didn't know the witch well but sensed she was annoyed by something. "How did you know about the missing woman at Casper Creek?"

Stormy looked exasperated by the question. "I told you. It's all over the news."

"And how did you watch the news? I don't have a television. You were at the store when I left an hour ago. You didn't have time to catch a news program."

"The radio has news, too," Stormy pointed out. "I was listening while driving around."

"Were you following me?" Astra's tone was biting. "Is that how you ended up here?"

"Oh, don't flatter yourself." Stormy waved off the comment as if it were nothing more than an annoying fly. "I was looking for a cool place to visit. I happened to see this one on a map. It's purely a coincidence."

Hannah didn't believe that for a second. "And you just

happened to show up at the same time we did? That's quite the coincidence."

"Isn't it, though," Astra murmured. Hannah was no longer the focus of her attention. No, that honor was now bestowed upon Stormy. "I think we should talk about a few things."

"Oh, sure. I love talking about things," Stormy bubbled. "Whenever you want, I'm up for it."

"I think now is a good time."

Sensing it was time to leave, Hannah slowly stood and grabbed her shoes. She hadn't planned to hang by the river overly long anyway. She was just waiting for the deputy to take the dog and move to another spot so she could test her magic and try to find a trail that led to Heather. It was the only thing she could think to do.

"Well, it was nice to see you again," Hannah said blankly as she stood. "I need to be on my way. I'm sure you and your friend will have a ... nice ... afternoon. I hope to see you again."

"Oh, you'll definitely see us again," Stormy called out. "You have something that belongs to us."

Astra's eyes flashed with outright hostility. "Me." She thumped her chest for emphasis. "She has something that belongs to me. You're not a part of that equation."

"We shall see."

"Oh, we definitely will."

TWELVE

*H*annah made it to work on time. Her interaction with Astra — and especially Stormy — left her unsettled, but there wasn't much she could do about it until Cooper checked in. Even then, she was leery about telling him what happened. He would most likely give her a lecture about spending time with Astra while at the same time reminding her that there could be something dangerous lurking in the fields around the town. She was already aware of both of those things so there was no need to dredge it up.

Nick was in the saloon by himself when she arrived and he looked out of sorts.

"What's wrong?" she asked, instantly worried. She scurried around the bar to grab an apron. "Did something happen?"

"I thought maybe you guys were going to leave me here alone or something and I was freaking out," Nick admitted sheepishly. "I mean ... I had fun yesterday. I think I'm catching on. I'm not ready to solo it, though."

Hannah took pity on him. She hadn't considered that he might be panicking because she left her appearance until the last second. "I'm sorry. I was down by the river trying to help with the search. I didn't realize you would be here alone."

"I heard about that." For once, Nick wasn't cracking wise. "What's going to happen?"

"What do you mean?" Hannah was only half listening because her mind was on other things. Her attempt to use magic to find Heather had been an unmitigated disaster. Nothing she tried worked and she was feeling down on herself ... and more than a little frustrated. "What's going to happen where?"

"Here." He was earnest. "Are they going to shut things down because that woman disappeared up here?"

Hannah furrowed her brow, confused. "Who are you talking about?"

"The cops. They're all over the place."

"Ah." Realization dawned and she flashed a weak smile. "You don't have to worry about that. The police will keep searching for Heather because that's their job but we're not liable for what happened to her. They signed release forms saying exactly that, and Cooper and I stopped in last night to warn them about straying. They knew not to leave."

"Yeah, but ... they were drunk. I know because I served them some drinks before I left. They were more than halfway to tipsy when I finished with them and they had a bunch of their own stuff. They were probably hammered by midnight."

Hannah thought back to the interaction she shared with the women. "They actually weren't terrible. I mean ... well ... they weren't exactly sober. They were hardly tripping over their own feet or slurring either. Besides ... there's debate whether Heather wandered off on her own."

"I don't know what that means." Nick's face was blank. "What else could've happened?"

"Well ... ." Hannah hesitated. She wasn't sure how much

she should say. In truth, Nick was the one who spent the most time with Rick the previous day. If anyone had any insight into the man's mood, it would be her young companion. "What can you tell me about the time you spent with Rick yesterday?"

Nick looked surprised by the conversational shift. "Um ... I don't know. What do you want me to tell you?"

"I don't specifically want you to tell me anything. I'm simply curious about his mood. I mean ... was he angry? Was he sad? Was he happy?"

"I'm not really sure that guy is ever happy. Sure, he puts on a good act, but it's obvious he doesn't feel the bulk of the emotions he wears."

To Hannah, that was an extremely odd — and maybe a little profound — statement. "You're saying that he only pretends to be friendly."

"Oh, I don't know about that. I mean ... friendliness is one of those things that's not easy to gauge. I'm saying that he's not altogether right in the head. He puts on a good front, don't get me wrong, but I know how to recognize the signs of mental illness."

Hannah jerked her eyes in his direction. "Oh, yeah?"

He nodded, solemn. "My mother. She was mentally ill, to the point where she was locked up when I was twelve."

"I'm sorry. That must've been difficult to deal with."

"Yeah. I was in the hospital at the time because she locked me in the attic before she set the house on fire. I breathed in a lot of smoke and was weak. There was a time they thought I wouldn't make it. I was really out of it when they dragged her away and I thought it was a dream. I was terrified they were going to send me back to live with her."

Hannah's stomach constricted. "That is ... awful. I'm so sorry. I can't believe your mother tried to kill you."

"Yeah, well, she had issues." Nick forced a smile that

133

didn't make it all the way to his eyes. "I guess it was good that I was an only child. I took the brunt of her anger up until that day but there was no one else to protect me. I could escape to the woods and hang out with my imaginary friends – who were always women because I was a boss even then, mind you – when she was having an episode. It wasn't always so bad."

Hannah leaned against the counter, conflicted. She wasn't sure how hard she should dig into Nick's private business, but she was legitimately curious. "Where was your father?"

"I have no idea. I never met my father. It was just me and her. I'm guessing he left when he figured out she was nuts. I know I would've done the same."

"Still ... what happened? After, I mean. Who did you live with? You were only twelve, so living on your own wasn't a possibility."

"Honestly, I could've lived on my own at twelve." He wasn't bragging, merely matter-of-fact. "I'd been self-sufficient for so long I actually chafed when I went to live with my grandmother. She wasn't a horrible woman. I don't want you to think that. She was just ... limited."

Hannah had no idea what that meant. "How so?"

"She didn't really want to be a mother the first time around, but she got pregnant with my mother and had no choice but to get married. In her time, it was quite the scandal to be unmarried and have a baby. Of course, she admitted to me on her death bed that she didn't want to have my mother in the first place, but she couldn't find a place to have an abortion back then."

Hannah was officially horrified. "How could she tell you that?"

Nick shrugged, noncommittal. "She was blunt. I don't think she did it to be mean. It explained a lot, though. She didn't want my mother and she probably didn't hide that fact. The only reason she took me in was because she considered it her duty. She also said I wasn't much of a burden because I basically took care of myself."

Hannah wasn't sure how to respond. "That is still awful. I'm so sorry."

He cracked a smile. "Now that you feel sorry for me, can I take you to dinner?"

The shift was enough to throw her for a loop. "What?"

He laughed this time, his gregarious nature returning. "It's a joke. I've noticed, through the years, that if I tell my story to anyone I get a lot of sympathy sex. I probably shouldn't have tried the line on my boss, though. It was a reflex ... and I'm sorry."

Hannah managed to relax, although it took a great deal of effort. Because she sensed he needed it, she decided to play along with the game. "You should probably be careful talking about that stuff going forward," she agreed. "I would hate to have to write you up."

"And on my first week of work." He looked mournful. "Leave it to me to stick my foot in my mouth. As for the rest, I probably shouldn't have told you about it. I inherited that blunt thing from my grandmother. Actually ... I got a few personality quirks from her. It's not always a good thing."

"I don't think it's so bad." Hannah grabbed a rag so she could wipe down the counter. "Honestly, I'm impressed that you managed to survive what happened to you. I don't want to pry, but what happened to your mother?"

"She's still locked up in a mental hospital. She has delusions, like ... really weird delusions. Like, for example, she always told me when I was a kid that my grandmother was a black widow spider in human form. No joke. She suggested my grandmother was spinning a web to trap her in and intended to eat her at some point.

"Then, when I was like eight or so, she said that my father

was a vampire and tried to suck her blood so she staked him in the chest and hid his body in the backyard of the house," he continued. "She was paranoid to the point of being intolerable to be around. She would tell me things like my principal was a pervert ... and my teacher was a prostitute on the side. Mind you, a lot of the time I was too young to know what any of those things meant. I learned fast, though, because she described what she was talking about in excruciating detail."

"Oh, wow." Hannah brushed her forearm against her forehead. "I don't even know what to say to that. That must've been so difficult for you."

"It was just normal to me. I didn't realize it was abnormal until I got into middle school — I was home schooled until I went to live with my grandmother — and the other kids basically told me in no uncertain terms that the things I'd been taught to believe were utter nonsense. It was a hard lesson."

"I bet. Still, you seem to have turned out okay. Have you always lived in this area?"

"Most of my life," he admitted. "My grandmother is buried about twenty miles from here. I inherited her house, which is older but still nice. I've been doing some work on it."

"It sounds like you're very industrious."

"I like to keep busy." He shifted his eyes to the empty street. "The first wave should arrive in about twenty minutes, right?"

Hannah nodded. "You catch on quick." She remembered the original point of their conversation. "Back to Rick, though. Did he say anything yesterday that made you nervous? Did he say anything weird?"

"Like I said, he was a weird guy. I think I read people relatively well because of ... well, everything. He's clearly a little crazy."

"Can you expand on that?"

"Sure. He wants people to think he's sane and he largely covers for his dark thoughts. They slip through, though. Like, for example, that woman who died. I think you mentioned her first. He acted like he didn't care about her, but he brought her up a good five times after you left ... and he was happy she was dead. He didn't come right out and say it, but he basically thought it was karma because she dumped him, like she deserved to die simply because their relationship didn't work out."

Hannah swallowed hard. She'd been wondering about that. "Well ... that's weird, huh?"

"It's definitely weird," Nick agreed. He didn't seem bothered by the conversation in the least. Hannah figured that was a product of his upbringing. Nothing really fazed him because he'd already dealt with the worst life had to throw at him. "Where is he, by the way? Shouldn't he be here by now?"

Hannah flicked her eyes to the clock on the wall. "Yeah. He was due forty-five minutes ago."

"Did he call in sick?"

"No, but I'm starting to think he's not coming."

"So ... just you and me? That will be a hardship." He winked, causing Hannah to smirk. "It's a good thing you're pretty. Otherwise this day would totally suck."

"You're doing it again."

"What?"

"Flirting with your boss. That's a no-no."

"I'll try to refrain, although it will be difficult."

"Give it your best shot."

. . .

COOPER IMMEDIATELY HEADED TO THE saloon when he returned to Casper Creek. He was anxious to check on Hannah, and wouldn't be placated until he saw for himself that she was okay. To his relief, she was working behind the bar and seemed to be having a good time as the new bartender cracked a myriad of jokes, causing her to dissolve into numerous fits of laughter. For some reason, the scene bothered him.

"Who is the new guy?" Boone asked, joining Cooper on the street.

"Nick Something-or-Other," he replied, wrinkling his nose when Hannah lightly slapped the man's arm and broke out in gregarious guffaws. "He's local and just started."

"He seems to be a funny guy."

"Yeah, well ... ." Cooper made a face. "You don't think he's attractive, do you?" When Boone didn't immediately respond, he shifted his gaze to the spot over his shoulder and found the sheriff's shoulders shaking with silent laughter. "What? Why are you laughing?"

"Because you're jealous and I didn't think I'd ever see it," Boone replied, recovering quickly. "Seriously, though, I don't think you have anything to worry about. I've seen the way Hannah looks at you. She's already taken."

"I'm not jealous." Even as he said the words, Cooper realized they might not exactly be true. "I'm just ... looking out for her. She's the boss. It's my job to make sure she's safe."

"Uh-huh." Boone obviously didn't believe that for a second. "Are we heading inside? I want to touch base with her, see if she's discovered anything."

"Yeah." Cooper let loose a heavy sigh. "Don't tell her I was watching her. And, whatever you do, don't tell her I'm jealous. It will give her a big head ... and it's not even true."

"Your secret is safe with me." Boone clapped him on the shoulder before moving ahead. He was the first one to walk through the door and he fixed Hannah with a friendly smile. "How are things here? Anything?"

Hannah, rueful, shook her head. "No, and I've been watching." The smile she graced Cooper with was bright enough to warm him all over. "I was wondering if you were going to come back."

"I didn't plan on being gone so long, but we got distracted searching for Rick." On a whim, he moved directly to the bar and planted a quick kiss on her lips. It was the first time he'd put their relationship out there for the other workers, at least in such a direct manner, and he felt good about it when he pulled back. "I missed you, though."

"Oh." Nick bobbed his head in understanding as he took in the scene. "This makes sense. No wonder you didn't respond to my flirting. You've already got a boyfriend."

Hannah pressed her lips together in amusement as Cooper's eyes fired with annoyance.

"You've been flirting with my girl?"

Nick merely shrugged. "Hey, I didn't know she was taken. For the record, I flirt with everybody. That's how I rack up the tips."

"It's true," Hannah offered as she filled two glasses with iced tea and shoved them in the direction of the two men. "The women love him. He's got a special way with the customers."

"Keep it with the customers," Cooper warned, although he couldn't help smiling at the sheepish man. "What else has been going on? I assume, since I didn't get a text, that Rick didn't show up for work."

"Nope." Hannah shook her head, solemn. "He didn't call either. What's going on with the search?"

"Nothing so far," Boone replied, taking a seat at one of the stools. "We have three K-9 units out there."

"I know. I saw one of them when I headed down to the river."

Cooper's shoulders stiffened. "Excuse me?"

She realized her mistake too late to take it back. She hadn't meant to blurt it out that way. "Oh, um ... well ... crap."

"Yeah. What were you doing down at the river?" His expression was stern, which only served to make him more attractive, Hannah realized.

"I went for a walk," Hannah replied, refusing to be apologetic. "I had some things I wanted to think about. It's been a big few days and I had time to burn before my shift. Also ... I thought maybe I might be able to help in the search for Heather." She didn't say how she planned to help because Nick was standing next to her. "It turns out there was nothing I could do so it was a wasted effort."

"You didn't see anything?" Boone queried.

"No. Well ... I ran into Astra down at the river." Since she'd already told half the story, Hannah figured it was best to get the rest out of the way so Cooper could stew over it and get it out of his system. "She was hanging out and being her usual self."

Cooper's frown was pronounced. "Did you talk to her?"

"Yes, and she was fine. We didn't fight or anything. That new witch you mentioned, Stormy, showed up. You were right about her being weird ... and suspicious. She mentioned Heather's disappearance even though there should be no way of her knowing about it. Astra was not happy."

"I think Astra is realizing that Stormy is more witch than she can handle," Cooper mused. "Neither of them threatened you, did they?"

"No. I was actually down on the list of things Astra was worried about thanks to Stormy's presence. I think she was furious."

"Good."

Nick cleared his throat and drew three sets of curious eyes to him. "Who are Astra and Stormy?"

Boone chuckled hollowly. "It's a long story. I'll leave it to these two to tell it. I'm going to head back. We only have the dogs another two hours."

Hannah's heart dropped. "What happens after that?"

"I don't know." Boone drank the last of his iced tea and stood. "So far, the dogs haven't caught her scent. They're out there wandering aimlessly. If they don't hit soon ... well ... I don't think that's going to be good for anybody concerned."

"She has to be out there." Hannah was adamant. "I mean ... where else could she have gone?"

"She could've gotten in a vehicle and driven away," Boone replied. "The fact that Rick isn't here and yet he was supposedly here after dark last night makes me think that he's not only our lone suspect, but our best one. Why wouldn't he come into work if he was innocent?"

"I don't know." Hannah felt mildly sick to her stomach. "The whole thing is freaking me out."

"If Heather was taken like the other women — and I have no reason to think otherwise given her hair color and eyes — then we're dealing with one predator here," Boone explained. "Rick already has ties to June. Now he was seen with a second woman. I hardly think that's a coincidence."

"Do you think Heather is already dead? I mean ... she's supposed to get married the day after tomorrow." For some reason, that prospect bothered Hannah beyond all else. "Do you think there's still a chance we'll find her?"

"There's always a chance." Boone offered up a small smile. "June was alive for a full week after she disappeared. There's every chance that Heather is, too."

"That means there's every chance Heather will show back up and kill herself," Hannah noted. "That's basically what you're saying."

"We don't know what we're dealing with. We simply have no idea. Until we know otherwise, we'll proceed as if Heather is alive and hope we luck out."

"If you strike out with the dogs, what's your next step?"

"I honestly have no idea. We're going to have to think outside the box on this one. We might need the public's help to find Rick — if he's even still in the area — and that is likely to create a panic. We're honestly in uncharted terrain here. I don't know what to tell you."

"Well, great." Hannah rolled her neck and sighed. "That's not what I wanted to hear."

Boone shrugged. "Sorry."

Cooper reached across the bar and rested his hand on top of hers. "It's going to be okay," he promised. "We'll figure it out. How about, after the town closes, I bring dinner and we spend some time talking things over? That might make you feel better."

Hannah managed a smile for his benefit. "Sure. That sounds like a great idea."

"Good. I'll see you in a few hours ... and I'll make sure to have something you like."

"As long as I see you, I'll be fine."

Cooper grinned. "I feel the same way."

"Oh, geez." Boone made a growling noise from his end of the bar. "You guys are so sweet I have a toothache."

Cooper shot a dark look in the older man's direction. "Don't give me grief. It's already been a long day."

"I'll see if I can refrain."

THIRTEEN

$\mathcal{H}$annah split her afternoon working behind the bar with Nick and doing research on the victims. If he was curious about what she was doing between busy spurts, he didn't ask. He was a self-starter and spent his time stocking the coolers and wiping down the tables and bar during lulls. Hannah was impressed with his drive and knew he would be a good fit for the staff. Since Rick was now missing, though, that meant she would still have to train another person if she ever wanted to get out from behind the bar. Nick couldn't handle the entire shebang on his own.

By the time Casper Creek closed, she had a crick in her neck from staring at the computer for so long. Nick bade her farewell, cast a curious glance at the computer, and then disappeared. He clearly didn't care enough to ask the obvious question. Hannah remained in her spot another thirty minutes, until Cooper arrived with their dinner.

"Hey." He watched her for a beat, shaking his head when she finally lifted her eyes. She looked cross. "You don't exactly look happy to see me."

"Oh, no. I'm always happy to see you." She offered up a genuine smile. "I didn't realize how late it was."

"Are you hungry?" He held up the bags. "I got Mexican on a whim. I hope you're okay with that."

"It sounds great." She closed her computer and slid it into the bag on the floor and fixed him with a rueful look. "I meant to change my clothes before dinner so you wouldn't have to put up with me in my uniform, but I lost track of time. I can still head up if you don't mind waiting five minutes to eat."

He took a moment to study her in the outfit. "I hate to break it to you, darlin', but I happen to like the uniform."

"You're the only one."

"That's not even remotely true. Every man who has ever seen you in that outfit falls in love on the spot."

Hannah snorted, genuinely entertained. "I don't think it's love. I think it's lust." She gestured toward the cleavage that was on full display. "I'm more than my boobs."

He sobered quickly. "I know. I was just joking. I think you're much more than ... um ... them."

She was amused despite herself. "I'm still going to run up and change. Give me five minutes, huh?"

"Sure. I'll check on Jinx while I'm waiting. Do you want him here or with Tyler?"

"Oh." The question caught her off guard. "Um ... if he's having a good time, he can stay with Tyler. He'll be all over us while we're eating if we have him here."

"I'll make sure it's okay."

FIVE MINUTES LATER, HANNAH WAS DRESSED in comfortable knit pants and Cooper was back from checking on Jinx. They exchanged a sweet kiss before sitting to eat.

"Jinx is perfectly happy chasing the goats and Tyler says

he'll keep him for a bit," Cooper volunteered as he opened his burrito container. "He even said he would keep him overnight, but I figure you'll want to have him with you before bed. I told him we'd play it by ear."

"That sounds good." Hannah grabbed a container of sour cream and spread it over her burrito. She didn't want to dwell on serious things now that they had some time to themselves, but she couldn't exactly shove the missing women out of her mind. "I take it the dogs didn't find anything."

"No." His expression was dark. "I don't know what to think. The dogs couldn't find any trace of her outside the brothel."

"Arnie said he saw her walking on Main Street, though."

"He did, and even though he's older — and a little cantankerous — I believe he saw what he said he did. I don't know what that leaves us with, though. I mean ... it's possible Rick knocked her over the head and removed her from the scene, but I don't know how probable it is. He's not exactly a big guy."

"Heather wasn't very big either," Hannah pointed out. "She wouldn't have been all that difficult to lift."

"In theory, that's true. She would've been dead weight, though. I mean ... if we follow the theory that he knocked her out. Even drunk, I don't think she would've gone willingly, so being unconscious is our best bet."

"Not necessarily." Hannah used her plastic knife to saw into her burrito. "What if he convinced her there was something he wanted to show her in the parking lot? He could've waited to knock her out then. Heck, maybe he opened his trunk, she leaned over to look in, and he just shoved her in there. Like you said, she was drunk and her balance might've been off."

"I guess that's true. Why didn't the dogs pick up her scent walking in that direction, though?"

"I don't know. I'm not familiar enough with the way the dogs do things to hazard a guess on that. Maybe they simply missed it."

"I guess." He rubbed the back of his neck, his expression unreadable. "What were you working on when I came in? You seemed extremely intent on your computer. I expected you to be still cleaning up after your funny friend left."

She snorted and rolled her eyes. "Oh, don't be jealous." She poked his cheek and grinned. "I only have eyes for you. He's funny, but he has his own issues."

Cooper caught her finger and leaned in to kiss the tip. "I'm not jealous. Okay, well, I'm mostly not jealous. You guys seemed to be having a good time. I don't like other guys flirting with you."

"I didn't realize you were a territorial boyfriend. Astra never mentioned that, and she brings you up every single time we talk. She's definitely a territorial girlfriend."

He scowled. There was nothing he hated more than mention of Astra. "Astra is a whole lot of things that aren't healthy. As for being a territorial boyfriend, I don't really like that term. I don't believe you're my property or anything. I just ... feel protective of you."

"I guess there's nothing wrong with that."

"I'll try not to get out of hand." He flipped up her fingers and kissed her palm. "I can't guarantee anything, though."

Her heart stuttered at the earnest expression on his face. "As long as you do your best." She stared at him for a long time and then remembered her food was getting cold. "Um ... what were we talking about again?"

"Your new employee. Do you think he's going to work out? If not, we're going to need to get on the ball and hire someone new."

"I think he's going to be great. No, really. He's smart and doesn't need to be reminded to do things. He stocked the refrigerators without prodding after each rush. We're still going to probably need someone new to take over for Rick if I ever want to try anything new here, though."

He pursed his lips. "You could always order someone else to take over in the saloon while you sample the other roles. I mean ... you could make Becky and Nick work together. I think they might be a good fit. He likes to flirt and she desperately wants a boyfriend."

"Actually, that's not a bad idea. I'll give it some thought."

"Good." Cooper beamed. "That's what I like to hear." He shoveled a huge forkful of burrito into his mouth and thoughtfully chewed before swallowing. "You didn't tell me what you were doing on the computer."

"Oh, right." She shook her head. "I'm distracted today. I was researching all the missing women. I was hoping I would be able to find a common thread as to why they were taken, but the only thing I could find is that two of them were engaged, and three of them were in serious relationships. I'm not sure about the first woman. That's basically all I managed to find."

"You think their relationship status is the reason they were taken?"

She held her hands out and shrugged. "It's possible it's just a coincidence. I honestly don't know what to think."

"Well ... I'll mention it to Boone. It can't hurt to chase."

"Thanks."

The rest of the meal was spent focusing on other things, lighter things. By the time they were finished and had cleaned up the containers, there was a noticeable vibe hanging over the room.

"So, what should we do next?" Cooper asked.

"I don't know." Hannah glanced around. "I guess we could

go upstairs and watch television. We should probably get Jinx before then, though."

"Or ... we could do something else." Cooper's gaze fell on the jukebox against the far wall. "How do you feel about dancing?"

The question caught Hannah off guard. "I ... don't ... know. How do you feel about dancing?"

"As long as it's slow and I don't have to know any complicated steps, I'm fine." He smiled as he dug in his pocket for change, surveying the selections a long time before coming up with a melodic Ed Sheeran song. "May I?" He held out his hand in an ingratiating manner.

Hannah's cheeks burned with pleasure. "Um ... sure." She melted into his arms. Unlike with other men she'd danced with, there was no uncomfortable pacing issue at the start. They fell into the exact same rhythm, swaying together and staring into each other's eyes.

"I know this is going to sound corny but ... I really like spending time with you and I'm having difficulty remembering what it was like before you came here," Cooper admitted in a low voice. "You're the best part of my day. You're the first thing I think of when I open my eyes and the last thing I wonder about before I fall asleep."

Hannah's heart did a long, slow roll. "I feel the same way. I kick myself for it, though. I keep trying to remind myself that I didn't come here for this."

"Just think of it as an unexpected bonus."

"Yeah, but ... I got in trouble before because I made my life about a guy. That's not who I want to be."

"Your life doesn't have to be about me. I would never expect that. I want to be part of it, though. Also, I'm not that jerk you were engaged to. I'm me ... and I won't ever cheat on you. That's not who I am."

Hannah swallowed hard. "I know that. I think I knew that

the first time I laid eyes on you, although I'm not sure how. I need you to know that I would never betray you. That's not who I am."

He cracked a smile. "We both have relationship issues. Maybe ... maybe we should put those behind us and only focus on each other. I think we're going to get a different ending this time."

"I don't really want anything to end. I want a continuous adventure."

His smile widened. "Me, too." He leaned in for a kiss. It started sweet ... and soft ... and was full of yearning.

It turned into something else fast.

Before either of them realized what was happening, they were gasping and holding each other tight. They kissed so long that Hannah's lips felt raw when she finally managed to pull back and see the wild look in Cooper's eyes.

"Do you want to go upstairs?" It was a bold invitation, but it's all she could think about.

He didn't hesitate this time. He didn't try to be the charming guy who was willing to wait. He was being consumed and he could think of nothing else. "Oh, yeah."

She gave a little laugh as she pulled out of his reach and headed for the stairs. "Jinx can stay with Tyler tonight. Catch me if you can."

He was already moving before she disappeared into the stairwell. Sometimes things were simply right, and that's how he felt about Hannah. The time for waiting was done. All he could think about was moving forward.

It was time ... for both of them.

HANNAH WOKE TO A SENSATION OF warmth she hadn't felt since ... well, she couldn't ever remember feeling this comfortable. And safe. She felt safe, too. With the sunlight filtering in through the window and Cooper spooned behind her, his arms wrapped tightly around her, it was the perfect morning.

Then she stirred ... and the nerves took over.

"Good morning," he murmured, brushing a kiss against the ridge of her ear and causing a chill to go down her spine. "How did you sleep?"

She smiled at the question ... and then frowned when her mind drifted to the dreams that had plagued her once again. Even with Cooper as a distraction, she'd returned to the foggy dreamscape and argued with the invisible force who lived there. She distinctly remembered that ... and yet the specifics of the conversation were somehow out of her reach, as if the fog was affecting her memory.

"That wasn't a trick question," Cooper noted as he propped himself on his elbow, his gaze keen as he studied her face. "Are you okay? Are you regretting what ... happened?"

Hannah immediately started shaking her head as she shifted to face him. "No. That was ... amazing." Her cheeks colored under his studied gaze. "I mean ... it was really amazing. I don't want to give you a swelled head but, wow."

He laughed at her reaction, nipping in for a soft kiss. She was warm in his arms and he loved the way she felt as she wrapped herself around him. She was in shape, which meant she was muscular and strong. She was also soft. He wanted to lay in bed and marvel at how it was possible the entire day. Reality wouldn't allow that, though. They only had a limited amount of time together.

"I think it was wow, too." He kissed her again and wrapped her tight. "I wish we could stay like this all day."

"Me, too." Hannah ran her fingers over his stubbled jaw. She knew her hair was probably standing on end thanks to the way he ran his fingers through it the previous evening.

He, however, was absolutely breathtaking. "You're really pretty."

He coughed, slightly embarrassed. "I don't think guys are supposed to be pretty."

"That's not true. You're absolutely beautiful."

"That's supposed to be my line." He grinned, enjoying the way her eyes watched him. She was soft with sleep, but he was convinced she had to be the loveliest woman he'd ever seen. "I don't want to get up." He made a whining noise as he gripped her against him. "This is one of those days we should be able to spend in bed without any outside interference."

Hannah happened to agree but she was a realist. "We both have work." Her mind took a detour as she thought about the day ahead of them. "Everyone is going to know we spent the night together, aren't they?"

"Probably. Tyler has a big mouth. Arnie was out here, too. One of them is bound to say something ... and then word will spread. Does that bother you?"

She shook her head. "No. I'm more worried about you. You've worked with these people for years. I don't want you to feel uncomfortable if they start teasing you."

"Oh, they're going to tease me." Cooper was resigned to that. "It was totally worth it, though." He leaned in and gave her another lingering kiss. Now, even though the overpowering need had burned off, he was still hungry for her. Honestly, he couldn't get enough of her. Despite that, he was mildly angry with himself. "I'm sorry."

The apology caught her off guard. "Why are you sorry?"

"I meant to wait. I wanted to make it special, make it something to remember. I didn't mean to completely lose my head and chase you up the stairs like an animal."

His earnest expression was enough to make her laugh. "Do you hear me complaining?"

"No, but ... we haven't been dating all that long."

"You said it yourself. Sometimes things are just right. I'm not sorry it happened. Heck, I'm not sorry how it happened. I'll remember last night for as long as I live. If it wasn't good for you, though ... ." She purposely left the statement hanging.

"That's not funny." He dug his fingers into her sides and started tickling, enjoying the way she gasped and squirmed.

They sank into yet another kiss, this one needier than the last. They were well on their way to a repeat performance when a scream rattled the window.

"What the ... ?" Cooper reluctantly pulled away and lifted his head. "Did you hear that?"

Hannah chewed on her bottom lip and nodded. "You're not imagining it."

He slipped out of bed and moved to the living room so he could get a gander at Main Street. What he saw was dumbfounding ... and took his breath away.

"Oh, geez." He dragged a hand through his hair and spared a glance for Hannah, who had wrapped a sheet around herself before joining him.

"Is that ... ?" Hannah's mouth dropped open when she realized what she was looking at.

"That's a dead body on Main Street," Cooper volunteered. "And that screaming is coming from Becky. We have to get down there."

Hannah was already moving. As fun as the romance had been, the real world was beckoning. They were going to have to live in both worlds for the foreseeable future.

FOURTEEN

*H*annah and Cooper dressed quickly, throwing on the clothes they'd discarded during their haphazard rush through the apartment the night before. Hannah didn't even bother running a brush through her hair, which she was convinced looked as if birds had been living in it. By the time they hit Main Street, Arnie and Tyler had joined Becky by the body.

"Who is it?" Cooper asked as he finished the buttons on his shirt.

Becky jerked up her head at the sound of his voice and the shock that registered on her face was something otherworldly. "Where did you come from?"

Cooper ignored her and moved closer to the sprawled figure on the ground, his eyes going wide when he realized who it was. "Rick."

Jinx was with Tyler and he woofed when he saw Hannah. He did not, however, race to his mistress.

"Hey, buddy." She smiled at him, even though the expression was hollow. "How are you this morning? I'll get you breakfast in just a second."

"I already fed him," Tyler responded absently. "I figured you and Cooper might want to sleep in ... although you went to bed early last night." He made an effort at a wink, but it was weak.

"I'm sorry we didn't touch base with you," she started. "I ... ." Honestly, she wasn't sure what she should say. Rick being dead seemed to take precedence.

"Don't worry about it." Tyler waved off the apology. "I didn't figure I would see you guys again last night anyway. I'm just glad I was finally right and it actually happened."

Becky was prim when she found her voice. "Are you saying that Cooper spent the night here? Did he sleep on your couch again? I know he's done that in the past."

Hannah had no intention of answering that question given the circumstances. "That's a lot of blood," she noted as she moved closer to Cooper. "Was he stabbed?"

"Yeah." Cooper's mouth was a tight line. "Multiple times, too. At least three that I can count. That's his uniform, right?" He scanned the body from head to toe. "Does that mean he didn't change from when he was here the day before yesterday?"

"Or maybe he was dressed for a shift today," Arnie suggested. He was paler than normal but composed. "Was he on the schedule?"

Hannah nodded. "He was but after he didn't show up yesterday I just assumed he wasn't coming back."

"Maybe something else was going on," Tyler suggested. "Maybe he didn't have anything to do with this after all. Maybe he was grabbed at the same time as the bride and held until he was killed last night." He raised his head. "Did anybody hear anything? I went to bed around eleven and didn't hear a sound. None of the animals roused either, even Jinx."

Hannah reached out to stroke the dog's head — he'd

always served as a comfort to her — but the dog easily sidestepped her. When she shifted her eyes to him, she found he looked grumpy. "What's wrong with you?"

"He's having a bit of an attitude," Tyler replied. "He was antsy last night when I tried to get him to go to bed. He kept whining and staring at the saloon. I think he was waiting for you to pick him up."

Hannah felt indescribably guilty at the words. "Oh. I'm sorry, buddy." She reached out to hug him, forcing the dog to let her wrap her arms around his neck even though he was obviously reticent. Don't be mad, okay? We just ... lost track of things."

Tyler snorted, although the sound was alien in the early morning quiet. "That's a nice way of phrasing it."

"He's been dead for at least four or five hours," Cooper noted, his eyes busy as they zeroed in on Rick's hands ... and feet ... and then traveled back to his chest, where all the wounds were located. "That would've put it around two o'clock or so when he died. We were all asleep."

"We still should've heard something," Hannah pressed. "I mean ... he was stabbed. Wouldn't he have cried out when it happened?"

"One would think."

Becky was no longer fixated on the body. Her attention was placed squarely on Cooper ... and she clearly wasn't happy. "Just so I'm clear, were you asleep in the same room?"

Cooper pretended he didn't hear the question. "We might've heard if we were in the front bedroom, but you insist on sleeping in the back bedroom. You're going to have to take over Abigail's old room eventually. You know that, right? It's simply more convenient. There's a master suite, complete with a bathroom attached."

Hannah made a huffy noise. "I think it's rude. She's still here."

"And she can't use her bedroom. Maybe you guys could sit down one day and sort through the stuff. Abigail can tell you what's important and you can keep it but then take over the room. It's your apartment now."

"Your apartment to sleep in alone," Becky stressed.

Tyler made a noise that was halfway between a laugh and a groan. "Oh, geez. This is like a bad sitcom or something."

"I don't know a lot of sitcoms that feature bloody bodies at the center of them," Arnie pointed out. "What are we supposed to do about this? The town doesn't open for hours but ... we can't exactly have tourists running around when there's a body in the middle of Main Street. That's going to totally ruin the high noon showdown."

"We're not going to be able to open today." Cooper was grim as he dug in his pocket and retrieved his phone. It was only half charged because he'd forgotten it in the melee with Hannah the previous evening. "Casper Creek is officially a crime scene now. Boone is going to have to shut it down for the day."

It wasn't the news that Hannah wanted to hear, but she didn't see where they had a choice. "I'll start making calls to the workers, make sure the lift doesn't even get started today. We don't want any accidents." She started moving toward the saloon and then slowed her pace, her eyes landing on Cooper. "This isn't exactly how I saw our day going."

The smile he sent her was small but heartfelt. "Me either. It will be okay, though. Start calling the workers. I'll get Boone out here. We'll go from there."

BOONE DESCENDED WITH AN ARMY of deputies and a contingent from the coroner's office. He went straight to the body, cursed a blue streak so fierce that Hannah felt herself blushing, and then started barking out orders. She excused herself long enough to return to her apartment and shower. Jinx reluctantly accompanied her, and when he got to the apartment and found Cooper's coat on the ground he promptly picked it up, carried it to the corner, and buried it under a mountain of toys.

"You're going to have to get over it," Hannah noted as she pulled her hair back into a ponytail. There was no reason to get fancy today. She figured she would be stuck in town for the duration. "Cooper is going to be hanging around."

The dog sat on the floor next to her, his gaze dark.

"You're still my favorite," she reassured him, dropping to her knees. "You know I love you. I promise not to leave you at Tyler's overnight again. That wasn't fair and you were probably confused."

Jinx's tail thumped against the floor. It was only once, but it was a start.

"How about I keep you with me all day today, huh?" She was trying to appease him, force him to forgive her. "That way we can spend every single moment together."

His tail thumped again.

She grabbed the leash from the counter and affixed it to his collar, earning another mean stare. "I'm sorry. You have to be on a leash while the police are here. They're not going to be happy if you mess up their crime scene. I don't make the rules."

Jinx lifted his nose into the air as she led him out of the apartment. He was definitely in a mood.

Once on Main Street, she took a moment to watch the activity. It made her sad to see the town shut down the way it was but there was literally nothing she could do about it. She would have to go with the flow and suck it up.

Boone saw her standing at the sidelines and made his way over to her. "You didn't hear anything?"

Hannah shook her head. "No. I was down the entire

night. I didn't hear a single thing ... and I feel guilty."

"You can't let this shake you." Boone had a paternalistic streak when it came to Hannah. She was older than his daughter by a long shot, but they boasted distinct similarities. Hannah's sadness tugged on his heartstrings. "You didn't do this. It's not your fault."

"That doesn't mean I couldn't have stopped it."

"Yeah, well ... ." Boone's gaze dropped to Jinx. "He didn't hear anything either?"

"No. He was with Tyler last night."

"I thought he slept with you every night."

"Oh, well ... ." Hannah averted her gaze and tried to find something interesting to stare at on the horizon. "Last night was a special occasion."

"Special occasion? What do you mean?"

Hannah felt trapped in the conversation. "I had a different overnight guest last evening," she mumbled.

It took Boone a moment to grasp what she was saying. "Oh!" He licked his lips and shifted from one foot to the other, uncomfortable. "So ... you and Cooper spent the night together. I guess I should've realized that when he said he needed to run home and shower. It didn't occur to me that he was wearing the same clothes as yesterday."

Hannah was determined to rein in her embarrassment. She was a grown woman, after all. She'd done nothing wrong. "Neither one of us heard anything. I just ... don't understand. If he was stabbed in the chest, you would think he would've cried out."

"Yeah, well, that's not the only place he was stabbed." Boone turned serious. "His throat was slashed, too. He would've bled out pretty quickly. The thing is, there's not enough blood on the ground. I just don't understand."

Hannah was taken aback. "That looks like a lot of blood to me."

"You would think, but the coroner says there should be four times what there is. He was obviously killed here. We've searched the entire town for a secondary attack site. There's nothing. That means the blood was taken for a different reason."

Hannah didn't have to ask what that reason was. "Well ... great." She rolled her neck and clutched Jinx's leash tighter. "I'm going to head over to the seamstress shop to talk to Jackie. You don't need me for anything else, do you?"

"No. I'm good for now." He reached out to touch her shoulder before she could move too far away. "You can't blame yourself for this. It's not your fault. Just ... let it go."

"I'll try."

Jackie wasn't alone in the shop when Hannah let herself in. She sat at an antique sewing machine, a project in her lap, and talked to Danielle and Becky as she worked. She looked as troubled by the turn of events as Hannah felt.

"Any news from the street?" Jackie asked as Hannah sank into the only open chair. "Do we know how he died?"

"Badly," Hannah replied, glum. "He was stabbed in the chest but Boone says he was also slashed across his throat. I didn't initially see the wound because of all the blood."

"Yeah, that was a surprise this morning," Jackie noted. "I was already here when I got the call that we didn't have to work today. I figured I would get ahead on a few projects." Her eyes were keen as she looked Hannah up and down. "What else is bothering you?"

"What makes you think something is bothering me?"

"You've got one of those faces that can't lie. It's the same reason I know you and Cooper did the dirty last night. You're glowing even though there's a dead body in the middle of town and you can't stop yourself from frowning."

Hannah worked her jaw. "That was quite the mouthful, huh?" she said finally.

Jackie's chuckle was low and warm. "Are you going to tell me I'm wrong?"

"No. There is something bothering me." Hannah unclipped Jinx's leash so he could get comfortable on the floor. He was still suffering from a bit of malaise, but she was hopeful he would forget his annoyance relatively quickly. "Boone says there's not enough blood out there. He says there should be four times what there is."

Jackie cocked an eyebrow. "And?"

"And what happened to the blood? Why is some of it missing? Does this have something to do with the goat?"

"What goat?" Danielle queried, confused.

"Tyler had a goat get out of the paddock the other day," Jackie replied. "He found it dead along the path between the town and the river. I didn't realize the goat was drained of blood, though."

"Yeah. That's what Tyler says at least," Hannah supplied. "He says that it was completely drained. Of course, he also says there were what looked to be bite marks on the back of the goat's neck. I assumed that meant an animal did it."

"There are different kinds of animals," Jackie noted, thoughtful. "It's also possible the blood was taken as some form of ritual. There are any number of blood rituals that need gobs of blood to carry out."

Hannah rubbed her palms over the arms of the chair. The coven witches were veritable fountains of information. She always learned something new whenever she spent time with them. "What kind of rituals?"

"There are a vast number of them. When you're dealing with dark magic, blood is almost always required. Most of the time we're talking about a prick of the finger, or maybe a small vial. When you get to the really big spells, though, then you have to go through a lot of blood."

"Can you give me an example?"

"Sure. There's one spell to stave off death that requires a sliver of your soul and eight pints of blood to be sacrificed."

Hannah did the math in her head. "That would most certainly result in the death of someone if the blood was taken from a lone individual."

"That's part of the spell. It takes a great sacrifice to give yourself eternal life. Only those darkest and most depraved would ever attempt such a spell."

Hannah's mind immediately went to Astra. "Do you think there are witches in the area who might try it?"

Jackie didn't bother to hide her amusement. "Is that your roundabout way of asking if I think Astra is capable of casting that spell?"

"I don't want to point fingers or anything but ... she's close, and she's aware things have been going on. Of course, when I asked her about crossing the boundaries, she denied it. She didn't seem all that concerned about the goat. She was intrigued, though."

"Was she surprised about the goat?" Danielle asked.

"Yeah. Either that or she was acting. I think she was legitimately surprised, though. She was distracted that day and wasn't putting on her usual show. She has a new witch in her coven, a woman named Stormy. She's mouthy and all kinds of trouble."

"Then maybe she's the witch behind this," Jackie suggested.

"We don't even know we're dealing with a witch," Hannah argued. "There's another side to all of this. There's the missing women. I think this is all linked, although I'm not sure how."

Becky stirred for the first time since Hannah had entered the store. She'd been listless and disinterested in the conversation up until this point. "Are you talking about the missing women on television? How could they be part of this?"

161

"Because Rick was seen with Heather Clarke the night before last. Arnie saw them together. Then Heather disappeared and Rick didn't show up for work. Earlier in the day, Rick admitted to me and the new guy — Nick, who is altogether delightful and I think you should make an effort to get to know, Becky — that he dated the third woman who went missing, the one who jumped off the bank building the other night. So, he had ties to two of the women."

"He's dead, though," Danielle pointed out. "He obviously can't be behind this if he's dead."

"Yeah. I know." Hannah rubbed the back of her neck. "I still think this all ties together. There has to be a way to figure out what's going on. Maybe the women were taken because whoever is doing this has a really big blood ritual they want to do. Maybe they need multiple people."

"And you think whoever it is needs to hold these women and kill them at the same time?" Jackie queried.

Hannah held out her hands and shrugged. "Maybe. I mean ... it's not out of the realm of possibility, right?"

"I guess not." Jackie was thoughtful. "What about the woman who jumped, though? Where was she held the week she was missing? Why did she jump instead of run for help?"

"I don't know. The coroner found a strange substance in June Dutton's blood. Maybe it was a drug of some kind. Maybe she was hypnotized and forced to kill herself or something."

"Okay, but why kill her in that manner if you need blood? Doesn't that break apart your entire theory?"

"Actually, it does." Hannah was loath to admit it, but there was a gaping hole in her logic. "None of it makes sense. I just can't wrap my head around it."

"We could try to do a mystical seance," Danielle suggested. "I mean ... there's no way of knowing if it will work, but we could try. There's no harm in making the attempt."

"What's a mystical seance?" Hannah was legitimately curious. "How is that different from a regular seance?"

"In a regular seance you want to talk to a ghost, or draw a soul from the other side. A mystical seance is when you want a specific location to give up its secrets. In this case, we would try to make Main Street show us what happened to Rick."

"Is that a possibility?" Hannah was eager at the thought. "I mean ... could we really do that?"

"We need some items before we can attempt it," Jackie replied, thoughtful. "The biggest is sage dust. It takes a month to make. Astra might have it at her shop, though." Slowly, she slid her eyes to Becky. "Instead of hanging around and pouting all day, why don't you head over to the shop and see if you can find some, huh? That will at least give you something to do."

Becky folded her arms over her chest. "I'm not pouting. I'm just ... not feeling well."

"Because you're pouting." Jackie was firm. "It's worth a shot. Head over there and see if you can find some." She flicked her eyes back to Hannah. "That's basically all we can do right now. I don't know a magical way of discovering the truth of what's happening to those women. We have to focus on the one thing we have control over, and that's Rick. He has to be our main priority."

Hannah couldn't argue with that. "Okay, well, keep me posted." She got to her feet. "I think I'm going to head back to my apartment and see if I can find any information on blood rituals in Abigail's books. With the town shut down, I don't have much to do. I might as well make myself useful."

"I think that's a great idea." Jackie enthused. "Stop in again in a few hours. I'll know more then."

FIFTEEN

*H*annah caught sight of Becky on Main Street when she was leaving Jackie's shop. The young woman stood next to the police tape and watched as they removed the body, something forlorn about her expression.

Even though Hannah was at the end of her rope with the young woman, she still felt sorry for her. She understood why Becky was struggling. It was hard to reconcile the world you thought you deserved with the one you ended up with. On a whim, Hannah crossed to her.

"Hey."

Becky made a face when she realized who was addressing her. "What do you want?"

Hannah bit down on her frustration and forced herself to remain calm in the face of the young woman's rudeness. "I know that things haven't gone how you expected them to go," she started.

"How I expected them to go?" Becky's eyebrows flew up her forehead. "Are you kidding me? This isn't about what I expected. This is about how things really were going until you showed up."

Hannah feigned patience. "And how is that?"

"Cooper and I weren't together before you showed up. I'm not an idiot and I don't think that or anything, but the groundwork was laid. All he had to do was look up and see what was directly in front of him."

Hannah licked her lips as she debated how to respond. Finally, she shook her head and sighed. "I don't know what you want me to say, Becky. Cooper and I are together. I don't see that changing. Even if we weren't together, though, I don't think you're his type."

"Oh, really?" Becky turned haughty. "Why is that? Do you think you're the only one who is his type?"

"Not even remotely." Hannah was calm despite the annoyance racing through her. "This has nothing to do with me somehow being special. It's just ... chemistry is a weird thing. There are plenty of people who should have it on paper who don't in real life. It's not a big deal."

"That's easy for you to say." Becky was bitter and there was no shaking her of the anger plaguing her ... at least at this time. "You got what you wanted. You got what I wanted. You've managed to steal him. You should be happy."

Hannah pressed the tip of her tongue against the back of her teeth and reminded herself that Becky was young. She didn't realize how ridiculous she sounded. After a calming breath, she forced a smile. "You can't steal a person from another person. Do you want to know how I know that?" She didn't wait for Becky to respond, instead barreling forward. "I know because I was engaged to a man who slept with any woman who would show him five seconds of interest. He always blamed it on them, or a sickness, but the truth is he didn't love me. We didn't belong together."

"And you're saying that you belong with Cooper? Is that it?"

"I'm saying that Cooper and I fit, and whatever you want to believe, sometimes things are simply meant to be."

"Like you and Cooper."

"Maybe." Hannah didn't want to push too hard on the subject. She understood Becky wasn't prepared to listen. "Here's the thing, though, you need to adjust your attitude. I know you're upset but that doesn't mean I deserve your vitriol every time I turn around."

Becky rolled her eyes. "Here we go."

"You're going to listen for a second." Hannah extended a warning finger and forced Becky to meet her gaze. "You may not like me — and that's your right — but I still deserve a modicum of respect.

"I'm not asking you to be my best friend," she continued. "I'm not demanding that you suck up to me or pretend that we're on the same wavelength. What I am demanding is that you not be rude to me. I am your boss whether you like it or not and I'm not going to put up with the sass any longer.

"I get that you feel as if you've been hurt ... and disrespected ... and perhaps even done wrong by me. That's not the case, though, and you need to get your head out of your ass. Seriously, I mean ... grow up. You're not a child and you're not always going to get your way."

Becky's mouth dropped open. "I can't believe you just said that to me."

"I'm not finished either." She'd come this far. Hannah knew she needed to push through the rest of the way. Then it would be done. "You don't have to like me. You do have to show me respect. If you don't feel you can do that, it's time for you to find another job."

Something flashed in the depths of Becky's eyes. It didn't feel dangerous, but Hannah recognized the woman was on the edge of saying something she would most likely regret. She steeled herself for it.

"You're firing me?" Becky queried finally. "Are you actually firing me?"

"No. I will if you don't stop this, though." She sucked in a deep breath and gripped Jinx's leash tighter. "You can't treat me like dirt. I won't put up with it. I understand and accept that you're upset. I will continue to treat you with respect. I won't sit back and be a walking doormat, though."

"Well ... that's just ... ." Becky muttered something under her breath that Hannah couldn't quite make out. It hardly sounded complimentary.

"Think about it," Hannah suggested, shifting Jinx's leash to her other hand. "You don't have to go to Astra's store to pick up the sage dust. I'll do that. I want to talk to her anyway."

Becky balked. "But Jackie told me to do it."

"Tell her I said that I wanted to do it. Astra and I need to chat and you have some thinking to do. If you decide that you can't do as I've asked, then I'll give you a few weeks' severance and you can leave tonight. Just ... give it some thought."

"Fine." Becky threw her hands in the air. "I'll think about it. Are you happy?"

"Not even close. If you're going to stay, the attitude has to go. No joke. If you keep talking to me this way, I will fire you. Make no mistake."

"Whatever." Becky scuffed her foot on the ground. "Is that all? Can I go now?"

"Yeah. Knock yourself out." Hannah watched the dejected woman trudge away and wondered if she'd approached the situation in the right way. There was no way of knowing until Becky settled, she realized. After that, she would have to gauge the situation. That would have to wait, though. Someone needed to visit Astra's store, and it only made sense that she should be the one to do it.

One fight down. One to go.

ASTRA'S STORE HAD UNDERGONE A FEW changes since the last time Hannah visited. She was impressed when she saw the buffed hardwood floors, and the counter area was new and shiny. Astra wasn't behind the register, which didn't surprise Hannah, but the new witch was.

"Stormy, right?" Hannah forced herself to remain calm under the haughty glare of the other woman. "You were at the river with Astra. Is she here? I need to talk to her."

"Why do you assume she wants to talk to you?" Stormy challenged, leaning against the counter and fixing Hannah with a dubious look. "I'm pretty sure she thinks you're a complete waste of time."

"That's her prerogative." Hannah refused to rise to the bait. "I'm actually here to buy something for a spell and I was hoping to steal five minutes of Astra's time. Can you please tell her that I'm here?"

"I think ... no." Stormy wrinkled her nose. "She said she didn't want to be bothered unless it was important. I can't think of anything less important than you."

Hannah forced a thin-lipped smile. "I think that should be her choice. Can you please just tell her she has a visitor? I promise I won't take up more than a few minutes of her time."

"I already told you no. In fact ... ."

The sound of a woman clearing her throat caused Stormy to trail off. When the witch shifted her eyes to the door behind her, she swallowed hard and then purposely blanked her face.

"Hey, Astra. You don't have to worry about this. She wants to see you, but I told her that you're only to be bothered for important things, which she's not."

Astra's expression was unreadable, but Hannah was almost certain she found annoyance there ... and it wasn't directed at her. Stormy was the one driving the white-haired witch around the bend.

"Thank you for looking out for me," Astra said dryly. "I think I can decide who I do and don't want to see, though. It's not up to you ... or for debate." Slowly, she tracked her eyes to Hannah. "Twice in one week. Things must be completely out of control at Casper Creek, huh?"

"They've been better." Hannah saw no reason to lie. "I was hoping you might be able to help."

"Yes, because that's exactly how I want to spend my day," Astra drawled. "Helping you will obviously complete me."

Stormy snorted to encourage her boss. "You tell her."

Astra's eyes flashed with annoyance, but she kept her attention on Hannah. "Why would I want to help you?"

"Because whatever is happening out there is bigger than both of us," Hannah replied, unruffled. She refused to let Astra bully her. If the woman wanted to laugh, shut her down, or even pick a fight, she would deal with the repercussions then. For now, she needed help, and she was worried Astra was the only one who could give it. "One of our workers showed up dead this morning."

"That sucks for you," Astra replied. "Who killed him?"

"I don't know. The thing is, he was seen with the bride who went missing the day before. He was the last person seen with her."

"So ... you're saying he's a murderer and yet someone murdered him?" Despite herself, Astra looked intrigued. "That's weird, huh?"

"I don't know that he was a murderer," Hannah clarified. "He was definitely our chief suspect. He had ties to the woman who jumped off the bank roof. She dumped him for another Casper Creek worker and he was bitter. Someone slashed his throat on Main Street last, night, though. Whoever it was managed to do it without waking anybody."

"Yes, well, I'm guessing you're a heavy sleeper because of all that air whistling through your head and Tyler has the cover of the animals in his paddock," Astra taunted. "If Arnie was out there — because he is sometimes — he's so old that he can't hear anything."

"Yeah, but Cooper didn't hear it either and he's trained to listen for things like that."

Hannah didn't realize her mistake until the words were already out of her mouth. The rage that flooded Astra's eyes was a thing to behold ... and then some.

"Cooper was there, too?"

Stormy sucked in a breath behind her boss. "Uh-oh."

Hannah refused to back down. "He was. He was asleep, though. We were all asleep. Nobody heard anything. Not only was Rick killed, but most of his blood was stolen. It's been suggested to me that someone might be trying to do a blood ritual and we want to do a mystic seance to see if we can ascertain who is doing this. I need some sage dust from you to carry out the spell, and I'm hoping you'll just sell it to me without offering up any grief."

Astra's anger was palpable. "I take it you and Cooper are getting even closer than you were before."

"That's really none of your business."

"Oh, but it is. Everything he does is my business."

Hannah shook her head. "It's not, though. You lost the right to care about what he does when you turned on Abigail. He sees that as a betrayal to him because he loved her."

"And does he love you now because you're a stand-in for her?"

"I don't think we're quite there yet," Hannah replied. "It doesn't matter, though. It's none of your business."

"Except it is." Astra's anger had teeth and she lashed out

with her magic, sending a blue bolt of hate in Hannah's direction.

Even though she was caught off guard, Hannah managed to react to the magic ... although it wasn't in a manner that anyone expected.

Instead of dodging, Hannah held up her left hand. The blue power surge, which was careening directly toward her, smacked into the palm of that hand ... and then exploded in a series of purple sparks as the red protection magic she'd somehow conjured without realizing she was doing it flared to life and beat back the attack.

Astra's eyes widened as Hannah's mouth dropped open. Neither woman had been expecting that outcome.

"What did you just do?" Astra barked.

"I don't ... know." Hannah stared at her hand. Her reaction had been instinctive, as if somehow she'd simply known what to do. "Hey!" Her eyes flashed as she focused on Astra. "You attacked me. I'm here to try to buy ingredients from you, and you attacked me for no good reason."

"Oh, I had a reason." Astra's countenance turned dark. "You're messing with things that shouldn't be messed with."

"Like what?" Now that she'd managed to show off a little bit, Hannah was feeling strong. "Cooper? Is that who you're talking about? You don't own him. Your relationship ended because you betrayed him. He won't ever overlook that."

"He doesn't belong to you," Astra hissed.

"He doesn't," Hannah agreed, making up her mind on the spot. She took a decisive step back. It was a mistake coming here, she realized. Astra was never going to willingly help her. On occasion, mutual need might have them crossing paths. The woman was never going to be a friend, though, and the sooner she accepted that, the better. "I don't happen to believe that one person ever belongs to another. That's not how to have a healthy relationship."

Astra barked out a hollow laugh. "Oh, now you're giving sermons on how to have a healthy relationship? That's ... rich."

"Not sermons. I just ... you know what? It doesn't matter." Hannah shook her head and started for the door. She was smart enough not to turn her back on Astra, though. She figured the dark witch wasn't above attacking from behind if her guard was down. "I shouldn't have come here."

"I think we can both agree with that," Astra said dryly. "I don't care about your problems at Casper Creek. They're not my problems ... until I take over that property. Then I'll care."

"That's never going to happen." Hannah was calm as she pushed open the door. "I may not be able to control much, but I can control that. I'll make sure there's never a chance for you to take over that land. I promise you that."

"Just go." Astra wrinkled her nose. "I don't want to even look at you."

"That goes double for me." Hannah was halfway through the door when Stormy decided to make her voice heard.

"We're going to take what's yours," Stormy warned. "We're going to take all of it, and that includes that fine man you're messing with. He's not yours, and we're going to take him back."

Hannah didn't respond. There was no need to. Astra, however, obviously couldn't contain herself.

"That property and that man are both mine," she snapped. "Who do you think you are?"

Hannah let the door fall shut, cutting off the rest of their argument. It had most definitely been a mistake coming here. She'd lived to tell the tale, though. That, at least, was something.

COOPER WAS HAPPY TO SEE RICK'S BODY had been

removed by the time he returned to Casper Creek. He was freshly showered, his phone charged, and he was anxious to see Hannah. She'd been in her apartment preparing for the day when he left. He thought he should say goodbye to her, but he didn't want to draw too much attention to himself from the workers who had managed to show up so he'd refrained. Now it had been more than two hours since he'd seen her and he was feeling antsy.

"Have you seen Hannah?" he asked as he stopped by Tyler's paddock, his eyes immediately going to Jinx. The dog looked less than happy to see him. There wasn't as much as a tail wag, although the canine's glare of disdain was firmly in place. "What's he doing here?"

"He is spending time with me because Hannah had an errand to run," Tyler replied, hoisting a bag of feed so he could transfer it to the barn. "He's grumpy, by the way. I think he thinks you're trying to steal his woman."

Cooper frowned at the dog as Tyler disappeared through the barn opening. "I'm not trying to steal your woman," he announced, holding Jinx's gaze. "I thought maybe we could share her."

Jinx didn't look impressed with the suggestion.

"I think we're both good for her," Cooper tried again. "I happen to care about her — and you — a great deal. We're going to have to compromise here. I promise not to leave you down here overnight again if you agree to play nice."

Jinx didn't blink.

"Come on now. There's no reason to be difficult."

Tyler chuckled as he returned to grab another bag. "No luck, huh? I think you're going to need to bribe him. He's mad ... and it doesn't help that Hannah took off and left him here again."

Cooper straightened. "Yeah. Do you happen to know where she went?"

"She didn't say. I saw her talking to Becky before she left, though. It looked like an intense conversation. Maybe she knows."

"Ugh. I would rather not talk to Becky."

"Is that because she loves you to the point of distraction?" Tyler teased.

"It's because she makes me uncomfortable. I ... ." Cooper trailed off when he spied Jackie walking in their direction. "Maybe she knows."

Tyler followed his gaze. "There you go. Jackie knows everything. She's also not a fan of talking to Becky unless it's absolutely necessary."

"Ha, ha, ha." Cooper mustered a smile for the approaching witch. He'd always liked her and found her sarcastic comments funny at the oddest of times. "How is life in the seamstress world?"

"Stressful," Jackie replied. "That's why I'm here. I'm looking for Becky. Have you seen her?"

Cooper slowly shook his head. "No. I was actually going to track her down, too. Tyler thinks she might know where Hannah is."

"Hannah ran to Astra's shop to get ingredients for a spell we want to do. I sent Becky, but Hannah intervened and volunteered to make the trip."

"Why would she do that?"

"Because she gave Becky something to think about before leaving," Jackie replied. "Basically she told her that she doesn't have to like her, but Becky does need to show respect. If she doesn't, she's going to be fired. That was the gist of the conversation."

"Well, I hate to say it, but that's a conversation that needed to be held weeks ago," Tyler noted. "I agree with Hannah on this one."

"I do, too." Jackie bobbed her head. "Still, Becky was in a

bad mood even when I told her Hannah was being more than fair. I wanted to check on her, but I can't seem to find her."

Even though he was agitated that Hannah would visit Astra on her own, Cooper was resigned to helping Jackie look for the missing member of her coven. "We'll check," he offered. "By the time we find her, Hannah should be back. I'm going to want to have a talk with her, too."

Tyler smirked. "It seems to be the day for it ... although I bet you wish you were doing something else with Hannah."

Cooper jabbed out a finger. "Shut up."

"Yes, sir."

SIXTEEN

*B*ecky hadn't been found by the time Hannah returned to Casper Creek. Cooper put together a small search party — they really didn't have a lot of people to choose from — and they scoured the town from top to bottom ... and came up empty.

Hannah found the group in the saloon when she returned.

"What's going on?"

Cooper jerked his eyes to her, relief mixing with annoyance. "Where have you been?" He already knew the answer, but he wanted to hear her say it.

"I went to Astra's shop because Jackie needed some sage dust for a spell. She wants to do some sort of mystic seance so we can see what went down on Main Street last night. Becky was supposed to go, but I volunteered to do it for her. It didn't go well."

Cooper's frown became more pronounced. "What does that mean?"

"It means that Astra has an attitude and I should've realized she would never willingly help. Stormy was there, by the way. She's still annoying."

Cooper shook his head. "Why did you go without me?"

"Because you weren't here. Besides, I didn't realize I needed a bodyguard."

"Astra has it out for you."

"Because of you. I know. She figured out you spent the night last night because I have a big mouth and she's not happy. She actually tried to attack me with magic." Hannah missed the way Cooper's eyes fired and barreled forward. "This really cool thing happened, though. She fired blue magic at me — I have no idea what type or anything, but I think it was probably wicked — and my hand automatically went up and deflected it. I swear, it was like my body knew what to do."

Cooper strode to her with a purpose, his hands sweeping over her shoulders and midriff. He was intent. "Are you hurt? Do you have pain anywhere? Tell me what you're feeling."

"I'm feeling annoyed." Hannah pulled away from him, her eyebrows drawing together. "I just told you I protected myself."

"And I want to make sure you're okay."

"Isn't my word good enough?"

Tyler, who had been watching the interaction with amusement, raised his hands and stepped between them. "Let's avoid any bloodshed, okay?" He was calm, but it was obvious he was keen to take charge. "Everybody is okay. There's no reason to freak out." His gaze was pointed at Cooper.

"She could've been hurt," the security chief protested. "Astra is a trained witch. Hannah has basically stumbled into her powers. I'm not saying she's not tough but ... Astra is better."

Even though she knew he was simply speaking the truth,

the words were like an arrow through Hannah's heart. "Well, if Astra is so much better, what are you doing with me?"

"Oh, don't do that." Cooper wagged a finger. "I didn't mean it like that and you know it."

"You said it." Hannah folded her arms and averted her gaze, opting to focus on Jackie. "What's going on here?"

"Becky is missing," Jackie replied succinctly. "We can't find her anywhere."

"Yeah, well, we had a talk," Hannah hedged, shifting from one foot to the other as discomfort washed over her. "I might have laid down the law with her."

"What does that mean?" Tyler asked, laying a hand on Cooper's shoulder to calm the other man. "I don't understand."

"I just ... well ... she's been kind of snippy with me." Hannah felt off her game. "She's had attitude because of Cooper, and I just explained to her that it wasn't fair and that she needed to get over herself. If she didn't think that was possible, I offered her severance but said I wasn't going to put up with her being rude."

"I think that's more than fair," Tyler said reasonably. "I'm being serious. You've put up with a lot more than most people would. You didn't do anything wrong. I was aware you had a talk. I was just checking to make sure nothing else happened that we weren't aware of."

Hannah risked a glance at Cooper and found him watching her with unreadable eyes. "I just didn't want things to be uncomfortable. I was in a good mood despite the death and destruction that seem to be hanging over this place and ... maybe she took off because she was upset about what I said."

"I don't think so," Cooper replied. "Her car is still in the parking lot. She's just ... missing."

Hannah pressed her lips together, considering. "Do you

think that she was taken? I mean ... someone has obviously been hanging around town without us seeing him or her. Maybe Becky was kidnapped or something."

"That's what we're worried about." Cooper dragged his hand through his hair. "I think we need to split up and start searching outside the town. We should do teams."

"I'll go with Tyler," Jackie offered. "Danielle can stay back here in case she returns. That leaves the two of you."

Cooper held Hannah's gaze and nodded. "We'll take the pathway toward the river, check the caves, and go from there. You guys hit the other side of town. Be careful and don't take any unnecessary risks. If you see anything of note, call me."

Tyler nodded without hesitation. "We can do that. She's probably just wandering around pouting. It's not easy to get over a crush."

"I hope that's all it is."

HANNAH AND COOPER LEFT TOWN together in relative silence. They'd only exchanged a handful of words since Cooper called Astra better, and the emotional distance between them was torturous.

"I'm sorry," Cooper offered in a low voice as they set off down the path. "I didn't mean that the way you took it."

Hannah was quiet for a beat, and when she did finally speak, it was with a remote tone. "Maybe that's how you feel."

"No, it's not." Cooper wanted to kick himself. "I didn't mean that Astra was a better person than you. I didn't mean that I think she's better for me. I just meant ... she's a stronger witch. That's not a bad thing either. You're still learning."

"She's definitely more knowledgeable," Hannah agreed, refusing to make eye contact. "She knew exactly what she was doing today and I only reacted out of instinct." She broke off and licked her lips, slowing her pace. "The thing is, maybe my instincts are stronger than her evil plans. Have you ever considered that?"

"Yes." Tentatively, Cooper reached out and grabbed her hand. "I think you're amazing. I think you're strong and you're going to be ten times the witch Astra is. I'm just ... afraid. Astra thinks in a way you don't."

"And how is that?"

"That wasn't an insult," he chided when he saw the grim set of her mouth. "You're a good person. She's not. Don't you understand that? She will react in ways you wouldn't dream of because you're not evil."

Hannah thought about the way she couldn't turn her back to Astra as she left. She understood — at least on the surface — what he was saying. That didn't mean she wasn't still hurt. "You think Astra is better than me."

"No, I don't." Cooper's frustration came out to play. "I don't think anybody is better than you." He moved closer and put his finger under her chin, forcing her to look directly into his face. "Right now, Astra has the upper hand because she's willing to hurt people to get what she wants. You want to protect people. That's always going to make you vulnerable.

"For her, magic is second nature because she's been practicing a really long time," he continued. "You only found out that magic was real two months ago. You've only been practicing a few weeks. She's only better on the magic front for now because you're still learning. When it comes to the rest of it ... well ... she lags so far behind you it's impossible for you guys to even see one another."

He was so earnest Hannah found some of the resentment she'd been hoarding like gold dissipating. She let loose a heavy sigh. "I don't want you with me because you think you should be. If you feel differently ... ."

"I don't." He swooped in and planted a hard kiss on her lips, fervently hoping she would give up the argument and return the sentiment. He wasn't disappointed. She sank into the exchange, melting against him, which allowed Cooper to slide his arms around her and hold her flush against his chest.

The kiss was torrid, to the point of taking them both over. They were breathless when they finally pulled apart, and Hannah had a feeling that they would've taken things in the other direction if they hadn't been standing in the middle of nowhere, with the only things to cushion them being scratchy grass and a rutted walkway.

"That was ... ."

Cooper smiled at her bewildered expression and leaned in to give her another kiss. This one was soft and brief. "That was a fine way to make up."

"I didn't realize we were fighting."

He laughed at the statement. "I'm not a big fan of fighting. It's inevitably going to happen, though. I think that should definitely be our preferred method of making up."

"I just thought we would get naked and roll around in my apartment."

"That, too." He gave her one more kiss and then pulled back. "We're okay, right?"

She nodded.

"Good, because we need to focus on finding Becky." Cooper returned his attention to the problem at hand. "She's a complete and total pain in the behind, but I'm worried enough about her being out here that I think we have to keep looking."

"No, I agree."

They started walking again, although this time their

fingers were linked. Because he couldn't bear the idea of being mired in silence again, Cooper was determined to keep the conversation going.

"What did Astra say when you fought off her attack so easily?"

"She seemed surprised."

"I bet."

"She also seemed a little ... worried." Hannah's forehead wrinkled as she thought back to the minutes following the attack. There hadn't been time to dwell on them before. "She really wants the Casper Creek property, to the point where she's becoming obsessive. She's obviously told Stormy what she wants with the property, too, although we're still in the dark."

"I've given that a lot of thought," he admitted, his eyes sharp as they searched the bushes and foliage for signs of movement. "I think there's something hidden on the land that she wants. Or, at the very least, she thinks there's something hidden here that she wants."

Hannah was intrigued. "Like what?"

"That I don't know. Maybe she thinks there's a magical well underneath the town, or a talisman hidden somewhere. Maybe she thinks Abigail purposely hid things away from her while she was here. Or maybe the land itself somehow acts as a booster for magic. You seem to be reacting to it."

Hannah pursed her lips. "I just thought it was one of those things where I heard about magic and then started manifesting. Is that stupid?"

"I don't know that I like that word," Cooper hedged. "I don't know how to answer that question. I'm not magical. You're the one going through this. What do you feel?"

"After last night — and that kiss we just had — I wouldn't sell yourself short on the magic stuff. That's what I feel."

His grin was lightning fast. "Thank you. I'm being serious, though."

"Who says I wasn't being serious?" When he didn't respond, she let out a long sigh. "It's hard for me to know what I feel," she admitted, sobering. "All of this is so new to me. Then, when you add you to the mix, my heart is always humming. I've never really had the chance to sit down and try to suss out the intricacies of this whole thing."

"Aw." He squeezed her hand. "You make my heart hum, too."

"I wasn't trying to be romantic."

"Well, you managed it all the same. Perhaps you're gifted beyond my wildest dreams."

"More gifted than Astra," she muttered under her breath.

"Oh, let's not turn this into a thing." Cooper sounded pained. "Please, I'm begging you to let that go. I really didn't mean it the way you thought I did."

Honestly, at her core, Hannah knew that to be true. It was time to be the bigger person, she decided. "You're off the hook. I'm not going to bring it up again."

"Thank you."

"I bet Astra would bring it up again."

"Oh, geez."

Despite herself, Hannah smiled ... and then turned serious. "Maybe we should look over there." She turned her head to an outcropping of rocks. She was familiar with the area, although she'd only been here once before. It was the same spot where she'd tracked a demon ... and watched an evil child die.

"I was thinking the same thing." Cooper was serious as he squeezed her hand and started pulling her off the trail. "Neither one of us wants to go back to that cave, but I don't see where we have a lot of choice."

"It would make sense for us to find him now," Hannah

offered, her voice low. "Logan, I mean." She thought she would feel some distress when thinking back on the boy who tried to kill her. He was so bad he managed to keep a demon captive and terrorize the creature to the point where suicide was a better option than living under his control. "We have a reason to be out here. We have a reason to search the caves."

Cooper hesitated. "It might still be a little soon. We'll think about that later, after we find Becky."

Conversation was sparse after that. The closer they got to the cave entrance, the heavier the atmosphere began to feel. It was dread that Hannah felt when they reached the opening of the cave.

"Should we go in there?" she asked finally.

Cooper was conflicted as he glanced between her and the opening. "I think we have to, just to be on the safe side. Under normal circumstances I would demand you stay out here while I go inside, but I'm not okay with us being separated."

Hannah wasn't okay with it either. "So, we'll both go in together."

Cooper released her hand and dug in his pocket for his keyring. He kept a flashlight there. He moved her hand to his back belt loop and smiled encouragingly. "I want you to keep hold of me. I'll go slow. If I tell you to run, I want you to run."

"I'm not leaving you."

"If I tell you to run, I want you to run," he repeated, firm. "I can take care of myself."

"I can take care of myself, too," she pointed out. "We're a unit now, though. That means we take care of each other. We're both going into this cave together, and we're both coming out together, too."

Cooper opened his mouth to argue and then realized it was a wasted effort. She was going to do what she was going to do. She wasn't much different than him on that front. He either had to accept it or let it go ... and the latter wasn't possible.

"Just stick close to me," he insisted. "There's probably nothing in here."

"That would be nice, huh?"

Hannah wasn't a fan of dark and dank places. Memories of the last time she was in the cave were still at the forefront of her mind and she struggled not to think too hard about what had happened to Logan. Even more, she desperately tried not to think about the monster that lived inside of him. It was the stuff of nightmares.

She remembered the trek through the cave from when she was there before and her heart pounded the closer they got to the final chamber. She kept her finger around Cooper's belt loop as he insisted and did her best not to melt down even though she was suddenly feeling claustrophobic.

It wasn't the easiest endeavor.

"We're here," Cooper said on a whisper, lifting the flashlight above his head. He scanned the ground first, and Hannah didn't have to ask what he was looking for, especially when the beam hit the small figure curled on the ground.

Hannah's heart flopped when her eyes landed on the dead boy. He'd been bitten by a snake and left for dead, and she still wondered if she'd done the right thing. Knowing the evil he was capable of, though, was enough to give her at least a little peace of mind.

"Logan," she breathed.

"Yeah." Cooper lifted the flashlight higher. "There's no sign of your demon. I think he really did take off like he said he was once he was fully recovered."

"I'm glad."

"Yes. How weird is it to say that we were rooting for the demon in this one, huh?" His lips quirked as he swung the flashlight to a different wall, his heart threatening to stop beating entirely when the light bounced off a different set of eyes. "Holy ... ." He almost dropped the flashlight he was so surprised. At the last second, though, he maintained his grip.

Hannah felt all the oxygen whoosh out of her lungs at the sight in front of her. Three women, all blond, stood with their backs pressed against the wall. Shoulder to shoulder, they stared at the cave invaders ... and didn't say a word.

"I don't ... ." Hannah's voice was barely a squeak. She found she was so frightened, she almost couldn't find the words to say what was necessary.

"Heather?" Cooper asked after a beat, focusing on the blonde farthest away from them. She was the one he recognized from the conversation above the brothel. "Heather, can you hear me?"

The woman didn't respond. None of them did. They simply stood there ... and stared.

"We should do something," Hannah said, finally finding her courage as she released Cooper's belt loop and took a determined step forward. "We have to get them out of here."

Her words were enough to stir the women. They all moved at the same time, jerking their heads in unison until they were all focused on her, and then they started hissing ... like snakes.

"That can't be good." Cooper reached for her hand ... and missed. "We need to get out of here. Right now."

SEVENTEEN

"*We* have to help them."

Hannah was completely focused on the women. It never occurred to her that they weren't chained or restrained ... at least by any obvious method. She couldn't see beyond her excitement.

"Hannah, wait." This time when Cooper reached out to grab her he managed to make contact, wrapping his fingers around her wrist and jerking her back.

"What are you doing?" Annoyance positively rolled off Hannah in waves. "We have to help them."

"I agree. We need backup before we do, though." He gave her a firm shove toward the tunnel. "We'll get help and come back."

Hannah was honestly baffled by his reaction. "What are you talking about? They're right there."

"I know but ... ." As if somehow drawn magically to them, Cooper's eyes shifted back to the women. They were detaching from the wall ... and heading toward them. "Run. Right now. Run!" The shove he gave her this time couldn't be described as gentle and he was insistent as he moved behind her. "Don't look back."

"What are you talking about?" Hannah wanted to continue arguing, but the hissing noises coming out of the women had doubled in frequency. They were loud enough to send a chill through her, and when she risked a glance over her shoulder, she saw the glittery eyes staring as the women's mouths worked in unison. "I think they're trying to talk."

"That's great." Cooper was done playing nice. He grabbed her around the waist with one arm and dragged her into the tunnel, using his other to hold up the flashlight. Hannah struggled against his iron grip, but he refused to release her. Somehow, deep inside, he knew that would be disastrous.

"Cooper!" She fought for freedom, her mind rebelling against the idea of leaving the women behind. "What are you doing?" Through a small gap, she finally managed to get a good look at Heather's face ... and what she found staring back at her was the stuff of nightmares. The woman, her face drawn and pale, had what looked to be small snakes writhing under her skin. And the eyes, something Hannah found expressive during her brief interaction with the bride-to-be, were completely devoid of life.

"Run," Hannah ordered, immediately ceasing the fight and instead grabbing Cooper's hand to drag him forward. "Run."

"I believe that's what I just said."

The women followed Cooper and Hannah all the way out of the cave. When the sunshine finally hit her in the face, the relief Hannah felt was of the overwhelming variety. She tripped coming out, stumbling forward and landing on her knees with a loud groan. Cooper was immediately behind her and he turned, standing as a barrier between his fallen girlfriend and the ghouls in the cave.

He needn't have worried, though. The women stopped at

the threshold, refusing to leave the darkness and embrace the light.

"What's wrong with them?" Hannah asked as she rolled to cradle her knee. She'd smacked it hard upon falling. "Why are they like that?"

"I don't know." Cooper kept staring at the abominations, who continued hissing, almost as if talking to one another. When he was certain they wouldn't risk the sunlight, he dropped so he was on the same level with Hannah and began checking over her knee. "Are you okay? Can you walk?"

"I don't see where we have much choice." Hannah gritted her teeth as she pressed her hand to her knee. "I'll be fine. I might be a little sore tomorrow, but I should be able to make it back before it stiffens up."

Cooper studied her face for signs she was covering. "I can carry you."

"Two miles?"

"I can carry you." He was firm. "I've done it before ... and with guys who weighed a lot more than you."

His military service, she realized. He was telling her he'd carried his fellow soldiers out of hot zones. It was something she hadn't spent too much time thinking about. Now wasn't the time to dwell on it either.

"I can walk," she reassured him. "We have to get moving now, though. The longer we wait ... ." Her eyes traveled back to the hissing women. "What's wrong with them?"

"I don't know. We need help, though." He slid her arm over his shoulder and helped her stand. "I don't think they're going anywhere ... at least not right now. We need to get back to town and prepare."

"Prepare for what?"

"For what's to come, because I'm pretty sure this is nowhere near over. Now that we've discovered the truth, they'll be coming for all of us."

. . .

HANNAH MANAGED TO WALK THE ENTIRE way back to Casper Creek, even though an impatient Cooper offered to carry her another two times. Jinx yipped excitedly and vaulted through the paddock slats when he saw his mistress. It was as if he sensed she was in pain and the time for being angry was over.

"Don't give me that look," Cooper warned as the dog glared at him for the walk to the saloon. "I didn't do this to her. I'm trying to help."

Jinx kept his eyes on Hannah, fear present in the depths of his chocolate eyes.

"We'll take care of her together," Cooper promised. "We'll work as a team."

"What happened?" Tyler asked as they maneuvered through the swinging doors. He had a towel on his shoulder and had obviously been busy behind the bar. "Is she okay?"

"She's been better." Cooper led her to a chair and helped lower her in it, moving another chair close enough for her to elevate her legs. "Stay right there," he ordered before shifting behind the bar to gather ice. "Tyler, I need you to get everyone who made it today and get them here."

Tyler looked conflicted as he glanced between Hannah and Cooper. "Do I even want to know what happened?"

"Probably not, but you don't have a choice. Trouble is coming."

Tyler straightened. "How much time do we have?"

"I'm guessing until the sun goes down."

"Well, great. That's not ominous or anything." Tyler started for the door. "What about Boone? Do you want me to call him?"

"Yeah. Absolutely. We need as many bodies as we can muster out here." Cooper returned with a towel, ice cubes wrapped inside of it, and placed it on Hannah's knee. "Hold this here, baby."

Hannah did as instructed, her heart still thumping due to the excitement of their escape. "What are we going to do?"

"We're going to figure it out." He moved to stand and then saw the fear reflected in the depths of her sea-blue eyes. "I won't let anything happen to you." He leaned forward and kissed her forehead. "I promise I'll keep you safe."

Oddly enough, his words were like a salve to her. "I promise to keep you safe, too."

He barked out a laugh. "That will be our new mission in life, to keep each other safe." They held gazes for a long beat, only looking toward the swinging doors at the sound of footsteps. Jackie was the first through the door.

"Did you find her?"

Cooper shook his head. "No. We found trouble, though, and it's of the really odd variety."

He laid it all out, making sure he omitted nothing, and then waited for her response. By the time he was finished with the story, Danielle and Tyler had joined them, and everyone was equally flabbergasted.

"Well, that's neat," Tyler said finally. "Who doesn't love a mindless woman who hisses like a snake and can't go out in the sun? I mean ... and people wonder why I'm gay."

"Nobody wonders," Cooper countered, shooting his friend a grin. "It is a problem, though, and we have exactly three hours to figure it out." His eyes landed on the clock. "I think it's fair to say that they'll be coming here once the sun sets."

"I think you're right," Jackie agreed. "I also think I know what we're dealing with."

"We're all ears."

"It's a snakeman."

Cooper blinked several times in rapid succession. "I'm

going to need more than that," he said finally. "I've never heard of a snakeman. I mean ... I like to think I'm up on the paranormal world but that's a new one for me."

"It's basically a boogeyman," Jackie replied calmly. "It's a monster that time forgot, the creature that lives under your bed, your worst nightmare."

Hannah involuntarily shuddered. "That sounds lovely. We didn't see a creature, though. We only saw the women."

"And you said they had snakes under their skin," Jackie supplied. "It's a snakeman. At least that's what they're called in the Voodoo culture. I think the technical term is a fallen incubus."

Hannah was taken aback. "An incubus? I've read about them. They're male sex demons. They kill women with sex."

Jackie bobbed her head. "That's it in a nutshell. That's a pure incubus, though. Sometimes they change. It's been theorized that they do this because of technology and shifting priorities in the world, but it hardly matters now."

"How do we fight it?" Tyler queried. "I mean ... what are we dealing with here?"

"They're all different." Jackie absently moved to Hannah's side and lifted the ice so she could get a better look. "I have a salve that might help with this." She tilted her head toward the door and caught Danielle's gaze. "Can you get my medical kit for me? You already know what I'm going to say anyway."

Danielle nodded without hesitation and slipped through the door.

"The snakeman probably didn't originate here. We would've heard about more disappearances if he did. Of course, he could've been born here centuries ago and only recently returned. That might explain how he knew where the cave was."

"Or he was drawn there for the same reason the demon was," Hannah countered.

"There is that, too." Jackie momentarily took on a far-off expression and then returned to the here and now. "The creature can be killed through magic ... or silver. We have swords locked away in the weapons chest. We're going to need to dole them out before dusk settles. We all need to be armed."

Hannah was chilled by the words. Still, she was curious. "What about the women? What's going on with them?"

"My guess is he poisoned them with his venom. This creature ... you have to understand, it looks human. It can pass for human."

"So it's probably someone we've seen," Cooper mused. "Anyone have any guesses on who?"

"I was leaning toward Rick," Hannah replied ruefully. "I guess I was off base there, though."

"What about the blood?" Cooper was desperate to get all the facts before the fight. "Why would this creature kill Rick and steal his blood?"

"And is this creature what killed my goat?" Tyler added.

"I think we can definitely blame the goat on him," Jackie confirmed. "As for why it killed Rick, I don't know. I'm not entirely familiar with the spell used to transform the women. My understanding is that the incubus can control certain people through magic ... and song ... and even in some cases, saliva."

Hannah wrinkled her nose. "Saliva? That's totally gross. I mean ... like totally gross."

Even though it was a serious situation, Cooper had to bite his lip to keep from laughing. He was beyond amused at her reaction. "Don't worry. I won't let him get his saliva near you."

"That would be nice. Although ... are we certain we're

193

dealing with a man?" Hannah directed the question to Jackie. "Couldn't the same thing happen with a succubus?"

Slowly, Jackie nodded. Her expression was conflicted. "In theory, yes. All the victims are women, though."

"Maybe we're dealing with a lesbian succubus. That has to be a thing. Sure, we haven't heard about it, but the percentages have to be the same, right? It's possible."

"I guess it is. Why is that important?"

"Because, if we're dealing with a woman, I have a suspect."

Cooper stirred and immediately started shaking his head. "It's not Astra. I know she's a sore subject between us right now — and I'm in no way taking her side — but it's not her. I would know if she was turning women into snakes. I don't think she could hide it."

Hannah snorted. "I wasn't actually talking about Astra, and I'm no longer sore about that. I'm just sore about this." She indicated her knee. "I'm going to have trouble moving against whatever is coming for us. I'm not going to be nearly as fast as I would normally be, because if it's a woman, I'm betting it's Stormy."

"Which is why you're not going to fight." Cooper kept his voice low. "I want you to lock yourself in the apartment upstairs with Jinx. The rest of us will fight this ... snakeman."

Hannah balked. "No way. I'm not going to let you fight without me."

"Hannah, you can't fight." Cooper was matter-of-fact. "Even if Jackie manages to work her magic, you're going to be hobbling. It's not safe for you to be out there."

"Well, then we're going to have to figure something out there, too." Hannah folded her arms across her chest, adamant. "I'm being serious here. You can't do it without me. You don't have enough manpower."

"There are three women and a snakeman. There are four of us — five if you count Boone — so we'll be perfectly okay."

"Don't forget Arnie," Jackie volunteered. "He's still out here, too."

"He has a gun," Cooper said, nodding. "That's good. He'll be able to lay down some cover. So, that's six of us. We'll handle it."

"Not without me, you won't." Hannah refused to back down. "I'm not going to just sit upstairs and hide while you guys are fighting. It's not going to happen. I'm part of this."

Cooper worked his jaw. "You are a complete and total ... ." He didn't finish the sentence. It would just lead to another fight, and they didn't have time for that. "What about the women?" Cooper turned to Jackie. "If we kill this creature, will they return to normal?"

"They should, although there's a tonic that couldn't possibly hurt. I have bottles of it stashed in the storage room at my store. It should restore the women quicker."

Hannah's mind was busy. "Then Heather could make it to her wedding ... and she wouldn't have snakes under her skin for the ceremony. It could still work out."

"There's something else to consider," Tyler interjected, drawing three sets of eyes to him. "Becky. We still don't know where she is. I'm assuming you didn't find her in the cave."

Cooper's heart skipped a beat. "No, we didn't. I completely forgot about her. It was freaky and we were in such a hurry to get back she slipped my mind. I'm guessing none of you have seen her either."

"She's gone," Jackie said. "Her car is still here, but she's gone. Either she's purposely hiding because she's pouting and wants attention, or she's been taken. I think there's a fifty-percent chance it goes either way at this point."

"What good would hiding do her?" Hannah asked, legitimately confused. "I mean ... what would be the point?"

"She might want to make it so Cooper miraculously finds

her," Tyler volunteered. "She might think that if he's worried about her, that means she still has a chance."

"She is delusional," Jackie agreed. "She's convinced herself that Hannah stole you from her." Her gaze was pointed at Cooper. "She thinks she had a legitimate shot."

"That was never going to happen," Cooper countered. "I mean ... never. It simply wasn't a possibility. She's a nice girl, but I wasn't attracted to her. It's nothing personal but ... that's simply the way it is."

"You don't have to justify yourself to me," Jackie reassured him. "I get it. Hannah is your match. I've known that from almost the first time I saw you two together. Even when you were with Astra, it wasn't a fit. You fit now."

Cooper spared a quick glance toward Hannah. "Even though the fit is going to be tight if she keeps putting herself in danger."

"That may be true, but we need her." Jackie opted for the pragmatic approach. "She's powerful and we're down a witch, one who might turn out to be working against us. We simply don't know what's going on with Becky. We have to proceed under the assumption that she's one of them."

"Then why wouldn't she be in the cave?" Hannah queried. "Why wouldn't she be with the others?"

"It could be that she was taken someplace else," Jackie replied. "She could be closer than we realize. Our snakeman might already be here. There are tunnels under this town. Don't forget that."

Cooper lifted his head. It was obvious the possibility hadn't occurred to him. "We have to stick to the plan," he said after a beat. "We can't risk going into the tunnels. We have to set up our defense here and work as a team. That's the only way we're going to be able to get through this."

"I agree." Jackie forced a smile for Hannah's benefit. "Are you going to be able to fight? I mean ... well and truly fight.

We need to take down the snakeman to save the women, and yet we're going to have to fight off the women long enough for us to kill the snakeman. It's going to be a balancing act."

"I'm ready." Hannah was grim. She understood the stakes. "What do you need me to do?"

"What you always do. Follow your instincts. They haven't led you astray yet."

Hannah could only hope this wouldn't be the first time.

EIGHTEEN

ackie's salve didn't exactly fix the issues with Hannah's knee, but it did numb up the area enough for her to walk. Cooper found her testing the injury in the saloon just as the sun started to set.

"I would still feel better if you'd go upstairs," he said in a quiet voice.

"Well, that's not going to happen." Hannah smiled when she turned. "I put Jinx up there. He's really mad, by the way. I think we're going to have to spoil him tomorrow ... if we survive, that is."

He frowned. "We're going to survive. I meant what I said. I won't let anything happen to you."

They both knew that was a promise he couldn't keep, but she opted to refrain from pointing that out.

"How do you think they'll approach us?" she asked instead. She wanted to be as prepared as possible.

"I think they'll try to split us up and isolate us. We can't allow that to happen. We need to stay together, as a group. That's why I'm here. It's time to group together on Main

Street. We're putting ourselves directly in front of the saloon. That means there are only two ways to approach."

Hannah nodded. That made sense. "The goal is to take out this snakeman — although I like boogeyman better, because snakes freak me out — and then, in theory, the women will return to their normal selves, right?"

Cooper understood what answer she wanted to hear, but he was hesitant. "That's the theory," he said finally. "If one of those women comes for you, though, you can't be afraid to take her out. We have no proof that this is going to work and you're more important."

"Than what?"

"Than anything, as far as I'm concerned. You're more important than what already might be dead."

Frustrated, Hannah placed her hand on her forehead. "I don't know that I can just kill them. We have to save them."

"We're going to do our best." He lifted the sword he carried. "This is for you. It's lightweight, so you should be able to wield it. Just be careful when you're swinging. You're not used to fighting with a sword."

"Is anybody used to fighting with a sword?" Hannah was rueful when she took the weapon. "I think I would prefer using my magic."

"This is just in case." He leaned in and gave her a sweet kiss. "I'm going to be right there with you. I promise. We're doing this together."

"Yeah ... and then maybe we can spend all day together in bed tomorrow, huh?" Hannah brightened considerably at the prospect. "We can even eat in bed. That's something to look forward to."

He nodded without hesitation. "That sounds like the perfect day."

"Even if Jinx is with us?"

"Yes." He was determined to get the dog to forgive him no matter what. He wanted to be with Hannah more than anything and the dog was part of the package. They would form their own little family and go from there. "Are you ready?"

She smiled and nodded. "Not even close."

He laughed at her reaction. "You're going to be okay. I'll make sure of it."

THEY GROUPED TOGETHER IN THE CENTER of town, everybody clasping weapons and standing so their backs were together. It wasn't a big group, but they were strong.

"What direction do you think they'll come from?" Boone asked from his place between Danielle and Jackie. He was grim, ready for a fight.

"I think they're going to come from multiple directions," Cooper replied. "That's why I thought this was the best location to take our stand. They can only approach from two directions, which cuts down on the potential for one of us being separated."

"That was smart."

Hannah stood between Arnie and Cooper, the former of whom was carrying a huge shotgun, which was apparently loaded with silver bullets. She found the entire prospect laughable but didn't give voice to her opinion.

She was antsy, fervently wishing that the attack would come sooner rather than later, when whispering started in the back of her mind.

I told you I would come.

She froze, her eyes jerking in the other direction, and she frowned when she realized a heavy fog was starting to roll in.

"What do you make of that?" Tyler asked, nerves on full display.

"It has to be coming from this creature," Cooper replied. "There was no fog in the forecast."

Arnie snorted. "Right, because forecasters are never wrong."

"It's him," Hannah announced, gripping the sword tighter. "It's definitely him. I ... he's here."

Cooper slid her a worried look. "How do you know that?"

"Because he showed this to me in my dreams."

A muscle worked in Cooper's jaw as he tried to tamp down the rising panic. She wasn't safe here. He knew that and allowed her to participate anyway. It was a mistake ... and now it was too late to force her upstairs to relative safety. "You're talking about the dreams you told me about. You just had them the one time, right?"

She shook her head as she met his gaze. "I've had them almost every night since this started."

"Even last night?" Frustration coursed through him when she nodded. "We were together last night. Why didn't you tell me?"

"So you could do what?" Her tone was practical. "What were you going to do? It was my head."

"And our boogeyman was invading it," Boone noted. "That probably would've been a helpful bit of information, Hannah. I'm not going to lie."

She made a protesting sound. "I didn't know."

On impulse, Cooper slid his free arm around her and gave her a tight side hug. "It doesn't matter now. We're in this and we're going to do the best that we can. We don't have any other choices."

She lifted her chin so she could stare directly into his eyes. "I'm sorry."

"Don't worry about it." He pressed a hard kiss to the corner of her mouth, jerking up his head when something hissed. The sound was closer than he would've liked. "They're here."

"Oh, you think?" Boone's sarcastic side was on full display as he gripped his sword and stared at a woman approaching through the fog. "Madeline Dwyer," he intoned. "She was the first one to go missing."

"That Heather woman is over here," Jackie called out.

Hannah flicked her eyes in that direction. "Don't hurt her unless you have to. I ... ." She trailed off when another figure appeared in front of her. This one she recognized, and the frozen eyes and pale skin were enough to make her blood run cold. "Becky."

"What?" Danielle shifted to see, but Boone slapped her arm to keep her in place.

"Focus this way," he ordered. "We have to keep in formation. We'll die if we don't."

Hannah's mouth was dry as she stared at the woman's face. Up until this point, she wasn't certain Becky was really one of the fallen. The dry goods clerk was petulant enough to hide like the others suggested, and then come out at the exact wrong time. It didn't look like that was the case this go-around, though.

"What's wrong, Hannah?" a male voice called out from somewhere behind Becky. "Aren't you happy to see your old friend?"

Cooper furrowed his brow as he shifted from one foot to the other. The snake women appeared to be in some sort of holding pattern, although it was anyone's guess how long that would last. "Do you recognize that voice?" he asked on a whisper.

That was a good question, Hannah mused. There was no doubt the voice was familiar, but where did she know it from? Then, a silhouette appeared in the fog. The creature was still a good fifty feet away, his features hidden, but Hannah knew.

"Nick."

He laughed in delight, clapping his hands. "I'm so glad you recognize me. This would be absolutely no fun if you didn't."

"Who is Nick?" Boone queried.

"The new bartender," Tyler replied. "I had no idea he was evil. It's too bad. He's cute."

"And a monster," Jackie added.

"That, too."

Hannah licked her lips and forced herself to remain calm. For some reason, knowing it was Nick she was facing off with had her feeling bolder. "I guess I should've guessed it was you." She was rueful. "You're the new element here."

"I did wonder if I was moving too soon given my position in this town, but I couldn't stop myself." Nick stopped walking when he was only a few feet away. His eyes gleamed an odd yellow color that made Hannah distinctly uncomfortable. They definitely looked like snake eyes. "I have compulsions that have to be fed."

"I bet." Hannah refused to give in to her fear and instead remained calm. "That story you told about your mother trying to kill you."

He was blasé. "What about it?"

"It was true, wasn't it?"

"I only told you the truth. I'm not a liar."

"You left out the part of the story where your mother wanted to kill you because you really were a monster," Hannah pointed out. "You made yourself the victim in the story."

"I *was* the victim," Nick countered, his eyes flashing with malice. "She was my mother. She was supposed to protect me. Sure, she obviously wasn't thrilled by what I was ... but that was hardly my fault."

"How did it even happen?" Cooper queried, drawing the odd creature's gaze to him. "How did a human woman give birth to you?"

"It was an accident really," Nick replied. He was unusually chipper given the circumstances. "My father went through a window to seduce her. One of the neighbors saw, and before he could finish his ritual ... well ... he was shot by some idiot who thought he was protecting my mother."

"Your father was an incubus," Hannah surmised, things coming together in her head. "He raped your mother but was killed before he could end her. That resulted in her being pregnant."

Nick's eyes flashed with malice. "It wasn't rape. Those women, including my mother, never had a word of complaint."

"That's because they were under his thrall and couldn't complain." Hannah felt sick to her stomach. "When did you find out what you were?"

"I think on some level I always knew," he replied calmly. "I always knew I was different. When I was a small child, I found I had control over people ... especially women. It was a fun game for me to play."

"And your mother recognized what you were," Jackie surmised. "She was already disgusted because you were the child of her rapist, but realizing you were different only made matters worse."

"So she said ... at least back then. She doesn't say much of anything anymore. She's locked up in a home. I tried to visit her when I got back to town — I've been away for a bit you see — but she freaked out and now the people at the hospital say I can't visit again. That's kind of a bummer because I love spending time with my mother."

"You mean you love terrorizing her," Hannah corrected. She still had questions, and even though she was ready to fight, she wanted her answers first. "How did you pick your victims?"

"I like a certain type of woman," Nick replied casually. "I prefer they have a certain ... aesthetic value. I've been traveling the last few years. That makes keeping off the radar easier. I land in a spot for a few weeks, have some fun, and then take off again. There's always been something inside that called me back here, though. Always."

"Yes, you were just a poor boy yearning for home," Hannah drawled. "What happened with June Dutton? Why did you kill her?"

"I didn't kill her. She killed herself. That's always what happens with my girls. I'm not sure why ... although I think it has something to do with the idea that they can't hold onto me forever and the reality of that is too much for them to bear."

Hannah rolled her eyes. "Whatever. Your ego is ridiculous. Something must've happened with June, though. The rest of them ... they're still here."

"I always like four," Nick explained. "It's a nice, round number. I like four friends whenever I'm in a place. I had planned to stay here longer — and I'm still considering it if tonight goes as planned — but I'm going to have to change up my girls a bit here and there so I don't get bored."

"That doesn't explain what happened to June," Hannah persisted.

"June, well ... she just wasn't a good fit. She kept fighting her condition. She shouldn't have been able to do it. All I can guess is that there was an abnormality in her body chemistry. She kept waking up and screaming at me. There's nothing I hate worse than a woman who won't shut her trap."

"The compound the coroner found in her body," Boone

suggested. "I'm guessing that he somehow controls them with that compound."

"I'm not even sure how it works," Nick admitted whimsically. "It's just something I've always been able to do. June was the first to put up a fight. She had to go. I dosed her hard and sent her on her way with a suggestion. I couldn't risk her returning to her life with grand tales of a monster who managed to control her mind, could I? Eventually, she might've been able to identify me."

"Yes, that would've been a true shame," Cooper drawled. "Why did you pick the cave on the bluff? Why did you decide to work at Casper Creek?"

"This place is magical," Nick replied simply. "There's an undercurrent of power here that simply cannot be denied. I felt it even when I visited as a kid. I was always drawn here. It was the first place I wanted to come when I returned ... and do you know what I saw when I came back?"

Hannah shook her head. "No. What?"

"You."

Her blood ran cold. "Me?"

"Yes, you were the culmination of everything I ever wanted," he explained. "You were powerful ... and sweet ... and oh, so pretty." His teeth gleamed in the limited light. "You had the strength to be my true match rather than a mindless zombie. You were obviously different, which meant I had to approach you differently.

"The plan was to seduce you, make you fall in love with me," he continued. "Getting the job out here was harder than I thought, though. It took weeks. When I finally did get it, you were already besotted with this idiot." He inclined his head toward Cooper. "I didn't think he would be an obstacle, but I turned out to be wrong."

Anger started growing inside Hannah at the words. The

notion that he planned on plucking her from her life and forcing her to be with him was infuriating. Because she still needed more information, she funneled her rage into the sword.

"Why did you kill Rick?" Cooper asked. "I mean ... what was in it for you?"

"It takes blood magic to keep my girls ... um ... happy," Nick replied. "He saw me with Heather that night and I was running dangerously low on blood after what happened with June. Sometimes animal blood can be used as a stopgap — sorry about your goat, by the way, but I was in a bind — but human blood is a necessity."

"You saw Heather that day in town," Hannah surmised, more power flowing to the sword. "You decided you wanted her. Why? Because she was blond, had blue eyes? That's your thing, right?"

"The heart wants what the heart wants."

His smug reaction filled her with even more rage. "Rick was there. Maybe he came back for some reason. He saw you with Heather and joined the party. Maybe he isolated her from you because he sensed something was wrong. That's what Arnie saw.

"Then you drew both of them away, probably to your cave," she continued. "You couldn't control Rick like you could Heather, so you decided to make him a suspect. That doesn't explain why you drained him before dropping his body on Main Street, though."

He held out his hands and shrugged. "I have a flare for theatrics."

"You just like attention, whatever attention you can possibly get." That's when Hannah realized that it didn't matter what he said. There was no explanation that would truly make her happy. There was nothing he could say that would comfort her when she tried to sleep tonight. Still, there was one more thing she needed to know. "Why did you take Becky?"

"Because I figured that would get you looking. I wanted to draw you away from the town. Away from him." He glared at Cooper. "The only time you've left this place is when you went to the witch's store and I couldn't very well approach you there. I would've been outnumbered, even if I wanted to control them all, and it was likely I would've been overpowered."

"You're going to be overpowered here," Hannah noted. "This is the end for you. You realize that, right?"

He snorted. "No. This is the end for them. It's the start for you and me. With you at my side, we'll be able to rule this place — this land — and draw power from it. Sure, we'll have a few key positions to fill after we kill them, but you'll be fine once you settle into your new life ... with me."

Cooper made a growling noise deep in his throat. "I won't let you touch her."

"You're not going to have a say in the matter." Nick was firm. "You're the first one I'm going to kill. In fact ... Becky, I think you know what to do." He smiled fondly at the hypnotized woman as she started moving in Cooper's direction. "I'm going to miss her when she's gone. After tonight, though, I promise to be a one-woman man."

That was it. Hannah couldn't take another word. She smoothly stepped around Becky, drawing herself up straight and tall in front of Nick.

"Don't worry," he reassured her. "This will be over quickly."

"It will," Hannah agreed, her smile sickly sweet. "It's over already. You just don't know it." With those words, she plunged the sword into Nick's chest. His eyes opened in surprise ... and fright. It was only then that he recognized his true plight. Hannah had a split second to wonder if he understood that his reign was over. Then, as he gasped and tried to wrap his hands around the glowing blade, her magic surged, building until it was practically a bomb that was set to go off. When it exploded, a bright light filled the sky. It was hot enough to burn away the fog, bright enough to turn night into day.

The last expression on his face that Hannah was able to register was one of resignation. He understood he'd lost ... and he was angry.

When the light blinked out, his body dropped to the ground. At the same moment, the hissing stopped. It was abrupt, the silence overwhelming, and when Hannah shifted she found Cooper holding an unconscious Becky in his arms. She'd fallen at the same moment Nick lost his life.

"Is she okay?" Hannah asked blankly, blinking as she tried to force herself to reality.

"She's going to be fine," Cooper answered automatically, shifting so he could swing her body up. "They're all going to be fine. Thanks to you."

"Okay. I need to sit down now, though. My knee really hurts."

He chuckled. "I think you've earned it."

NINETEEN

*H*annah was shaky when she moved to the bench in front of the saloon. She sank onto it, dropping the sword at her feet as the others grappled with the unconscious women.

"Hannah?" Cooper was desperate to get to her, but Becky was dead weight in his arms. Frustration overwhelmed him as he glanced back at the others. Everyone appeared to be occupied with the other women. "I'll be over there in just a second," he promised.

Hannah simply nodded. "Okay." She felt numb after what happened, and it was difficult for her to look in the direction of Nick's fallen body. She had no idea how long she sat in limbo because she lost track of time. When Cooper finally found her, she felt mildly disconnected ... although she offered him what she hoped was a pleasant smile. "That wasn't so bad, huh?"

"Oh, baby." He slid his arms around her waist and pulled her to him. "It's going to be okay," he whispered in her ear. "I promise it's going to be okay."

"Yeah." She rested her head on his shoulder as he moved

his hands up and down her back. "You did so good," he whispered. "I didn't even realize what you were going to do until it was already happening. I don't think he did either."

"I'm not even sure what I did," she admitted. "I was just ... angry. He was so entitled ... and terrible ... and horrible. I wanted him to shut up."

"Well, you shut him up." Cooper stroked his hand over the back of her head, feeling helpless when she began to shudder. "Oh, baby, don't shut down on me." He was desperate to keep her with him. "You were amazing. You did exactly what you had to do."

Hannah didn't doubt that. Still, taking a man's life — er, well, a monster's life — with her own bare hands was a new experience for her. She'd protected herself with magic before. This, however, was a more up-close-and-personal experience ... and she definitely didn't like it.

"I'm okay," she reassured him, patting his shoulder. "You don't have to worry about me. You should worry about Becky and the others."

"Tyler and Boone are taking care of them. I want to take care of you."

"I'm okay." It was an automatic response.

"You're not okay, but you will be. I promise." He kissed her cheek and pulled back, gratified to see some of the color returning to her angular features. His fingers were gentle as they brushed over her cheeks. "You did really well, Hannah." He knew he was laying it on thick, but he was impressed with what she'd managed to pull off. "I mean ... really, really well."

"Thank you."

He pulled her back and held tight, resting her head against his chest, glancing up at the sound of approaching footsteps. He wasn't surprised to find Boone watching them.

"Is she okay?" Boone asked, concern etching the lines of his face.

"She's okay," Cooper replied. "She's just ... overwhelmed. I think she'll be fine after a good night's sleep." He inclined his head to the four women slowly coming to their senses in the middle of the road. "What about them?"

"They seem mostly okay, if a bit dehydrated." Boone rubbed his chin, thoughtful. "I don't know if they remember anything. They seem cloudy on what happened."

"If we're lucky, they'll only remember the past few weeks in hazy dreams and assume it's their imagination working overtime. It's probably best if they don't remember anything."

"Yeah."

Hannah stirred, lifting her head. "How are you going to explain this to their families? I mean ... I'm sure everyone will be thrilled to be reunited, but this isn't going to be easy to cover up."

"It's easier than you think," Boone countered. "We have a culprit. He's dead. We'll just say that he was injecting the women with an unknown compound and controlling them with post-hypnotic suggestions. People will believe it because the outcome is exactly what they wanted it to be. Trust me."

"It sounds like you've done this before."

"Well, let's just say I've dealt with my fair share of the unexplainable." Boone rubbed the back of his neck and shifted his eyes back to the women. "I guess I need to call for an ambulance to have them transported to an area hospital to be checked out. I think they're okay, but I would prefer handing them over to a qualified professional."

"And what about Nick?" Hannah queried, her eyes going back to the body. "What will you do with him?"

"I'll send him in for a full autopsy because I'm curious,

and then I'll have him cremated. I'm willing to guess that he won't have people lining up to claim his remains."

Hannah pursed her lips. "What about his mother? She might not be as crazy as some people think. He really was a monster."

"I promise to check on her." Boone flashed a quick smile. "I can't make any promises, though. Either way, you don't need to worry about it. All you need to do is focus on yourself." He flicked his eyes to Cooper. "I'm guessing our friend here is going to be focusing on you, too."

"You've got that right," Cooper intoned, breaking into a legitimate grin as he held Hannah's gaze. "I see a lot of takeout in our future ... especially since we're spending the entire day in bed tomorrow. With Jinx, of course," he hastily added. "All three of us are going to lock ourselves away."

"That sounds great." Hannah managed a sigh and brightened. "I mean ... that sounds really great."

"It does. It's going to be part of our new normal going forward. I promise you that." He swooped in and gave her a soft kiss. "Did I mention you did really great?"

His earnest nature made Hannah laugh. "Maybe once or twice."

"I'm going to keep telling you because it was ... amazing."

"It was," Boone agreed, shifting away from the cuddling couple. "I'm going to ... head over there. You two keep doing what you're doing."

Cooper's grin widened. "That's the plan ... for the foreseeable future."

ON THE BLUFF OVERLOOKING CASPER Creek, Stormy stood and watched the scene play out on Main Street. She'd been there from the beginning, watching and waiting. She wasn't sure which faction would win ... right up until the point when Hannah had shoved the magically imbued sword into the creature's chest.

Stormy wasn't sure what he was. She'd never come across a creature like him before. She was, however, awed by what Hannah managed to accomplish. Apparently the novice witch was stronger than anybody had let on. That meant she was a bigger threat than Stormy initially envisioned.

That didn't mean she was too big of a threat to take down, though.

"Soon," Stormy muttered. "Soon this place will be mine, and there's no one who will keep it from me."